DW

W9-CSH-998

THE LAZARIDIS
MARRIAGE

THE LAZARIDIS MARRIAGE

BY

REBECCA WINTERS

MILLS & BOON®
Pure reading pleasure

All the characters in this book have no existence
outside the imagination of the author, and have
no relation whatsoever to anyone bearing the same
name or names. They are not even distantly inspired
by any individual known or unknown to the author,
and all the incidents are pure invention.

All Rights Reserved including the right of
reproduction in whole or in part in any form.
This edition is published by arrangement with
Harlequin Enterprises II BV/S.à.r.l. The text of this
publication or any part thereof may not be reproduced
or transmitted in any form or by any means, electronic
or mechanical, including photocopying, recording,
storage in an information retrieval system, or otherwise,
without the written permission of the publisher.

® and TM are trademarks owned and used by the
trademark owner and/or its licensee. Trademarks
marked with ® are registered with the United Kingdom
Patent Office and/or the Office for Harmonisation in
the Internal Market and in other countries.

First published in Great Britain 2007
Large Print edition 2007
Harlequin Mills & Boon Limited,
Eton House, 18-24 Paradise Road,
Richmond, Surrey TW9 1SR

© Rebecca Winters 2007

ISBN: 978 0 263 19500 2

Set in Times Roman 16½ on 19 pt.
16-1107-50654

Printed and bound in Great Britain
by Antony Rowe Ltd, Chippenham, Wiltshire

CHAPTER ONE

HE WAS HERE.

Though surrounded by the champagne-saturated party crowd aboard the Padakis yacht moored at Zea Marina in Piraeus, Tracey picked him out immediately.

Along with a bevy of exotic-looking women in elegant gowns, there were close to thirty formally attired business tycoons of various ages and nationalities talking over or gyrating to the loud music.

A portion of them were overfed and out of shape. Several stood taller and fitter than the rest. Some of that percentage still had their hair. A few had a whole head of black hair and an enviable olive skin blessed by the Mediterranean sun.

But only one man possessed all the gifts and had the shoulders of a Colossus too.

Nikos Lazaridis.

The sight of him in these surroundings sent a weakness through her body.

She'd first met him ten years ago through her grandfather, who was the head of Loretto's Mustard Company. If it hadn't been for him, she wouldn't have become acquainted with the brilliant entrepreneur from Greece. He'd been invited as a guest to the mansion in Buffalo where Tracey had always lived with her parents and grandfather.

After her father's death, from which she'd never recovered, she and her mother had tried their best to stay out of the way of her widowed grandfather who, like a bad king, demanded obedience.

If Tracey's grieving mother hadn't needed her support to deal with him, Tracey would have run away. Though he presented one face to the public, he was an evil man.

She never knew him to be intimidated by anyone, except when he talked about Nikos Lazaridis. In those moments Tracey heard envy, even jealousy, in his voice.

"In another couple of years he'll be worth more than our family ever thought of being."

"Why do you think that?"

"Have I ever told you the story of Helios, the sun god?"

"No."

"In 292 BC the Colossus was erected on the Greek island of Rhodes. It was a statue of Helios, roughly the same size as the Statue of Liberty, and one of the Seven Wonders of the World."

Tracey couldn't understand why he was telling her this.

"In *The Odyssey*, Homer called Helios the all seeing, all hearing. Even the goddess Demeter went to him for help in locating her daughter Persephone."

"Is that why you talk about him more than anyone else? Because he knows everything?"

"Yes."

She pondered his answer. "I thought you said *you* knew everything."

"I did…until I met him."

That day she'd learned Nikos had grown up in central Greece, the child of a poor farmer. A son whose sheer grit and brains had come up with an idea that had made history along with his fortune.

A week after the conversation, she accidentally met the man her grandfather had put on a par with Hellenic myth.

She'd been calling to her little black pug, Samson, who loved chasing birds. He'd been a gift from her beloved father before he'd been killed in a car accident.

As she rounded a corner to catch up with her dog, she discovered a man who was perfection. His height and coal-black hair made him different from any other as he stood outside the mansion with her grandfather. To her delight he was cuddling Samson, talking to him in endearing terms while being licked.

Paul Loretto didn't like children or animals, so her mom had helped to keep her pet hidden. To Tracey's horror, she realized too late her grandfather had come home early from the office with a guest. In front of this man, her grandfather scolded her unconscionably hard for not restraining her dog. It brought tears to her eyes, but he'd been too angry to care or even introduce her to the stranger.

If the visitor hadn't been there, her grandfather would have dragged her back into the house by the arm and locked her in her room. But the stranger had been there to prevent him from physically lashing out at her. He mitigated the pain further by flashing her a tender smile.

"You must be Tracey."

"Yes," she murmured, fighting not to let him see how hurt and humiliated she was.

"I'm Nikos Lazaridis. I met your mother last night. This little fellow is so cute, I just might take him home with me. I used to have a dog, too."

His deep-throated laugh of pleasure while he continued to play with Samson wrapped right around her heart.

"What kind was he?"

"A black-and-white mutt. I found him on the road injured, and took him home."

"What did you call him?"

"Zeus," he said, handing the dog back to her with care.

"The head god of Olympus."

His eyes flickered, as if he was pleased she knew something about the myths. "I named him that to make him feel important."

"Zeus was lucky *you* found him," she whispered.

Tracey's heart swelled as their eyes clung with an understanding she could feel on several levels.

He'd rescued his own dog from a terrible fate as surely as he'd rescued Samson from the wrath of her grandfather. Would that one day he might come from out of the blue and rescue Tracey.

After giving up the dog to her, Nikos's strong hands remained on her arms. He seemed to sense how frightened she was and wanted to protect her. The way he looked at her made her feel beautiful.

That was the day an awkward slip of a fifteen-year-old girl with long, embarrassingly red hair left unconfined, fell in love with the twenty-eight-year-old Nikos and worshipped him from afar. Silently, hopelessly, because after all, he was the Colossus of Rhodes come to life for her.

Since that fateful day ten years ago, there'd been more deaths; the tragic death of her precious Samson for whom she still grieved in her heart; the painful death of her innocence; the welcome death of her grandfather; the welcome death of her travesty of a marriage.

Most significant of all, the recent death of her mother, who'd succumbed to an aggressive form of cancer, leaving Tracey in the greatest pain of her life.

To the world, it meant she was now the major stockholder in the Loretto corporation. But all Tracey knew was that she was alone inside her soul.

"I'm afraid for you, Tracey," her mother had whispered near the end. "When you take my place at the next board meeting, they'll laugh at you behind your back the way they laughed at me. To them I was nothing more than a comical figurehead.

"Your business degree will do you no good unless you have something else up your sleeve that will make them sit up and take notice. You're going to need a mentor outside the company who will help you."

Tracey had figured that out a long time ago. "You mean like Nikos Lazaridis?" Though they'd only seen each other perhaps a dozen times in the three years before her marriage— always in the company of her grandfather— Nikos's name had come automatically to Tracey's lips.

"Yes, darling. I believe he's a man you can trust. Don't let what's happened with Karl scar you."

It wasn't what Karl had done. He'd been a

pawn in a game his father and her grandfather had engineered. She'd gone along with it to survive. Paul Loretto was the real culprit, but she'd held back certain information in order to save her mother the full horror of it.

"Have no fear, Mom."

Those were some of the last words they'd exchanged before her sweet parent had passed away.

If her grandfather knew what she was about to do right now, he'd climb out of his grave to stop her….

Tracey slipped a folded note to one of the young waiters circulating the deck with a tray of drinks. "Please give this to Mr. Lazaridis for me. Tell him I'll be waiting here."

He took the note, giving her the once over followed by a cheeky wink. "Of course, Ms. Loretto."

She held up some large bills for incentive. "Don't mention my name."

The waiter stared at the money, then back at her. "Do not worry."

Satisfied she'd made her point, she handed him the bills and watched him disappear to the other end of the yacht.

She knew he was bursting to tell everyone that the notorious Tracey Loretto with all her millions had shown up here to party with the legendary billionaire who, at the age of thirty-eight, continued to evade marriage.

No doubt the waiter's bank account would be further enhanced when he informed the press later on that she'd come hunting for husband number two.

With her mission accomplished and being utterly exhausted, she leaned against the railing on this hot June night, not seeing the lights of the Padakis yacht reflected in the harbor while she waited….

"*Kyrie* Lazaridis? Forgive the interruption."

Nikos excused himself from the conversation he was engaged in and turned to the waiter. "What is it?" he murmured.

"A very beautiful, exciting American woman waiting at the bow of the yacht asked me to give this to you."

As he stared at the folded paper in the young man's hand, Nikos's black brow lifted in speculation. "How much did she pay you?"

Nikos watched the other man's eyes light up. "Five thousand American dollars."

That much—

Though repulsed by the woman's tactics, he could understand the waiter's eagerness to accept such a large bribe. Once upon a time a young Nikos and his brother Leon had worked alongside their impoverished father to keep their small farm going. Back then, even a small portion of five thousand dollars would have changed their destiny.

Nikos switched from Greek. "Are you conversant in English?"

"I speak a little, *Kyrie*."

"Then read the note to me." Nikos couldn't bring himself to do it. The depths to which partying, empty-headed female predators sank revolted him. After he'd listened, he would tell the waiter what answer to give her that would send her packing.

Taken by surprise, the young man exhibited a blank look before he opened the flap.

"*H-Hail, Helios*," he began in broken English.

"*Hail, Helios?*" Nikos demanded in surprise, certain the waiter hadn't read it correctly. He took the note from him and finished studying it for himself.

Did you know my grandfather always called you that? The watchman of both gods and men. The first to see all things.

Nikos felt the impact of her words like a thunderclap.

Grandfather told me you're Olympia's spy from whom not much can be kept secret.

Thank you for the beautiful flowers. I'm sure Mother could smell their divine fragrance all the way to heaven.

Now that she's gone, I wonder if it's possible that you, who sees far and wide know why I've come?

A tight band constricted Nikos's lungs. Even after all this time, her reach was long and sure. She had no shame.

He put the note in his breast pocket for safekeeping. Wheeling around, the last thing he saw was the waiter's stunned expression as Nikos strode away, ignoring everyone waiting to talk to him.

Once upon a time Tracey Loretto had been like some ephemeral mermaid whose head appeared like a lick of flame above the waves for a brief moment, then recognizing she was spotted, darted off again, hiding her timidity and fear in the depths of the sea.

But that was before she'd grown up and developed land legs, finally understanding the kind of power she had over men.

If her mother's illness couldn't bring her to her parent's side in time to witness the separation of the spirit from the body, then what twisted bit of alchemy had been wrought for her to surface on Nikos's shore?

It was a dream he'd entertained until the day Paul Loretto had glibly told him that on her eighteenth birthday, he was giving Tracey away in marriage to Prince Karl Von Axel.

Being that the prince had been the twenty-five-year-old playboy son of a European family who had no money and nothing to offer Tracey but a defunct title, Nikos had felt the shock of that announcement like a mortal blow. He couldn't believe the Tracey he thought he'd known was capable of such poor judgment.

At that point Nikos had ended all visits to Buffalo. Any further business meetings with Paul, a hard, shrewd man, had taken place in

Athens, with no discussion of Tracey entering into the mix again.

The disastrous seven-year-marriage that had followed had given rich fodder to the tabloids. Nikos had watched her self-destruct from a distance. Every time the media had brought up her scandalous behavior, he'd thanked providence their paths had never crossed again.

Even before Paul's death, there had been problems within the Loretto company. Their quarterly earnings over the past few years had fallen. Division at the highest level had created instability, sending up a red flag.

Without her grandfather to pamper her, and no rich husband to support her extravagant tastes and whims, the ex-princess had turned her attention to Greece. In fear of her never-ending money source drying up one day, Nikos represented the ultimate safety net.

She'd come to target his wealth. Though Nikos was a commoner, ironically he had the lucrative trappings more than sufficient to keep her in the lifestyle her grandfather had provided from the cradle.

Nikos had news for her….

* * *

"Hail, Tracey."

Good. Her note had been delivered and digested.

She braced herself before turning to face the man she'd flown a long distance to see. When he spoke English in that deep, hypnotic male voice, his accent sent familiar vibrations beneath her skin, causing her pulse to race.

"I just flew in to Greece today."

"You do manage to get around. How was Monaco?" The sarcasm rolled off his tongue.

She swallowed hard. "I don't know. My friends went without me."

"I was sorry to hear about your mother. Now I'm afraid you'll have to excuse me. *My* friends are waiting."

He turned to leave, but she reached out and grasped his arm. It felt like steel. "Please, Nikos. Give me another minute. I'd like to talk to you."

His gaze glittered dangerously. "You made that clear with the five-thousand-dollar bribe you slipped the waiter. Once again you've let the whole world know you're Tracey Loretto who presents yourself like a gift to the world, even if you're not wanted or invited."

His words were as chilling as was the way he stared at her offending hand. She removed it from the sleeve of his immaculate jacket, but held her ground.

"Several weeks ago Giorgios Padakis sent my mother an invitation for this party. He wouldn't have known it was too late for her to attend, let alone enjoy it. So I came in her stead."

He eyed her through darkly lashed slits. "Why tell *me?* This isn't my party."

Tracey should have expected this reaction from him, but it hurt her so much she could hardly breathe. There'd been a time long ago when he'd treated her like something precious, but not anymore....

"The minute I heard you'd come to the mansion with those flowers, I felt terrible that I'd missed you, and wanted to thank you in person."

"Did you," he said in a wintry tone.

"Yes." She rubbed her moist palms nervously against the simple black material covering her hips.

"Then you've achieved your objective." His hauteur was unbearable.

All she could see were his broad chest and

shoulders. She had to tip her head back to examine the aquiline mold of his facial features. Beneath luxuriant black hair and brows, Nikos's eyes gleamed gold like the feral sheen of a panther's.

The male gods would have reason to be jealous of this particular mortal's gifts. No wonder her grandfather had been envious.

It didn't surprise her Nikos was studying her with such intense distaste. Before getting on the plane, she'd had her long red hair cut and styled to frame her heart-shaped face. She'd liked the color on her father, but not on her. In order to tone it down, she'd instructed the hairdresser to apply a tint.

Now that her mother was no longer alive, Tracey didn't feel guilty about it.

"Where did the mermaid go?" Nikos's voice grated, sounding far away just then.

Mermaid?

With that question, she couldn't imagine what he was talking about. But it was evident he didn't care for the change in her appearance. Not that it mattered. Her main concern was that she'd offended Nikos by not seeing him when he'd come to New York last week to pay his respects.

Ignoring his question she said, "I asked the staff to tell everyone I couldn't see people. But if I'd known you were coming to Buffalo, I would have made an exception."

His cruel smile devastated her. "Save your lies for someone who believes you. Everyone knows you were thousands of miles away from home."

She struggled to keep her composure. "You shouldn't believe everything you hear in the media." Tracey had planned to fly her mother there for a short trip, but she'd taken a sudden turn for the worse. "At the last minute I changed my mind and didn't leave her bedside."

His face closed up. He flatly didn't believe her. Oh Nikos—

"She was so ill at the last, she didn't want any visitors or a funeral. Her wish was to be privately buried in the family plot next to my father. No eulogies, no one except the hospice people and help from the mansion. I followed her dictates to the letter."

It was the plan she and her mother had devised to shield her from the members of the board, men like Vincent and David, as long as possible. But she hadn't been left alone long. How swift the vultures had been to gather, just as her mother had predicted.

"Diana Conner was a lovely woman. She reminded me of my mother. A real lady is rare."

And I'm none of those things, is that what you're saying?

There'd been a time in the past when Nikos had had the ability to make Tracey believe she was the only person of importance in the world. If he'd been jaded or bored, he'd given nothing away around her. That was his lethal charm, and one of the secrets of his phenomenal business acumen. But right now he was eyeing her with a quelling frigidity that seeped to her insides.

"It's only been a week." His words could have been a hiss. "The partying never ends for a creature like you does it?"

Creature? she moaned.

No one but Nikos could say that to her and make her bleed.

"I came to ask a favor."

"I'll just bet you did."

"But this may not be the appropriate time," she kept on talking. "I'm sure the woman you escorted to the party is growing impatient for your company."

He clasped his strong hands with their long lean fingers in front of himself, as if he needed to do something with them. "You paid the waiter to find out if I was alone tonight. Don't waste your energy denying it, Tracey. I see through you."

If he was here alone, then it was his choice. A man like Nikos used a party like this to conduct business. What he did with a woman would be in private.

It was incredible he hadn't married before now. It seemed no woman was important enough to give her his name. Or, he'd lost the one woman he could never replace.

Whatever the case, Tracey was here on a mission, and wouldn't allow herself to get side-tracked about his personal affairs that didn't concern her. She'd come for business reasons and nothing else.

"I didn't know if I would even find you here. Since you're such a busy man, you could have been out of the country. The second I saw you onboard the yacht, I thought I'd better make my move while I had the opportunity."

"Diana Conner was always gracious to me. She's the only reason I'm speaking to you now. Say what you have to say."

Tracey hoped the high round neckline of her cocktail dress with its diamond choker hid the throbbing nerve at the base of her throat. "When you find out what I want, I hope for Mother's sake you'll consider my request."

Lines bracketed his mouth, darkening his imposing countenance. "Go on." He was in a mood. Any second now and he would leave her in the dust.

Tracey fastened her eyes on him. Sea foam green her mother had called them, another physical trait inherited from her father.

This was it. She'd formulated an unorthodox plan, but the stakes were high. If she hesitated now, she would never get the courage again.

"In a word, I need your expertise." Her voice shook. "Would you be willing to let me pick your brains for say the next six months?"

The noise of the crowd and the music made the

silence emanating from him that much more pronounced.

She'd managed the impossible. Nikos Lazaridis at a loss for words. Maybe a good sign. Maybe not.

"With my mother gone, I'll be taking her place on the board."

Even with the distance separating them, she felt his body tauten.

"That ought to be interesting, provided you could tear yourself away from one of your playboys long enough to find the time to drop in."

His cutting remarks stung. But after the way the media had diced her up into tiny pieces, she shouldn't have expected any other reaction.

"Your comment is exactly the kind of bias I'll have to face from the board whether totally deserved…or not." His jaw hardened visibly. "If I want the rest of the members to take me seriously, I need to be taught how to make a meaningful contribution. That's what I'm after."

The ominous quiet that followed caused the hairs on the back of her neck to prickle. When he finally did speak, it was more like a grating sound.

"Why pick on me?" By the tenor of it, her

request was abhorrent to him, but she wasn't about to back down now.

Looking him straight in the eye, she said, "My grandfather said you were the only man he ever knew who didn't inherit, marry or steal your wealth. He feared you for that. I'm sure his board fears you even more."

Again she could tell she'd taken him by surprise. That wasn't a normal occurrence where Nikos was concerned. Anything but. She needed to strike while she had his full attention.

"If I were to become your protégée, so to speak, the men who've surrounded him will be too intimidated to trifle with me or shut me down during the meetings. With you as my unseen mentor, I *know* I could emerge as something better than the labels they've attached to me."

He folded his arms. "I'm sure one of them is dying to take you on as their trophy wife. Why not make a play for him and be done with it?"

Nikos had put the question out there, his way of throwing down the gauntlet. He really hated her. Since nothing else was working, maybe she could get that hate to work to her advantage.

"With Grandfather's death, and now Mother's, I own fifty-one percent of the shares in the company. For your help I'll give you fifteen percent. Together we would hold the controlling interest."

In an instant, a forbidding aura descended. "I guess I'm not surprised you think you can buy anything. But if you imagine I would touch one penny of your money, then you never knew me at all."

She lifted her gently rounded chin higher. "Has Helios so surpassed Midas in wealth, he can afford to ignore a billion dollars?"

"How did you come up with that figure?" he bit out, evading her question.

"David Hascomb." David was one of the junior attorney's in the law firm that handled her grandfather's affairs. He'd been pursuing her more vigorously since her divorce had become final two months ago.

"Actually that's an old figure. Since your grandfather's death, your company worth has already been reduced by two hundred million dollars. But I don't suppose Mr. Hascomb wants to alarm you until after he has rushed you into a second marriage."

Her grandfather had been right. Nikos knew everything.

Avoiding any talk of his reference to David's intentions, she said, "I'd like an opportunity to succeed at Loretto's.

"If you'll take me on, you'll discover I'm a fast learner. However, I can understand that six months probably sounds like an eternity to you."

She bit her lip. "At least it would be six and a half years less than Karl had to put up with me." Poor, lost, heartbroken Karl.

His eyes scrutinized her savagely, as if he were looking for something he couldn't find and was angry about it.

"You'll have better luck if you appeal to Vincent Morelli. He owns ten percent of the shares. I have no doubts he'll be more than eager to take you on as wife number three. But he'll have to sell some of his stock in order to get out of his second marriage."

She sucked in her breath. "Vincent Morelli is a revolting man who's made in my grandfather's mold. After mother died, he phoned and told me I didn't need to attend the meetings. What did I know about business?

"His exact words were 'Why don't we get together one night next week and I'll give you a personal account. That way we can enjoy ourselves and you won't need to bother your pretty little red head about anything.'"

"You ought to take him up on it," Nikos said with alacrity. "He may not have a title, but at least he comes with some substantial monetary backing. Even better, he's one of your grandfather's chief picks."

By now her whole body was trembling. "I would never allow that to happen again."

"Again?" Nikos demanded.

"My Grandfather was a tyrant. With Dad's help, Mom was able to stand up to him. But after Dad died, she didn't have the strength of will to fight my grandfather. As long as she did exactly what he wanted, we managed. However, one hint of rebellion and that was a different story.

"It was because of him I—"

Tracey stopped talking because she could tell she would never be able to reach Nikos. He was a force she should have known better than to contend with. Whatever kindness he'd once displayed toward her, she'd blotted her copy book to the point he despised her.

"I *what?*" he fired, not willing to leave it alone.

"Nothing. It doesn't matter. Thank you for remembering my mother. I won't forget. Goodbye, Nikos."

She turned to leave, but this time *he* was the one who caught hold of *her* arm so she couldn't move. "You've succeeded in gaining my attention. Now explain what you were going to say."

It was too late for Tracey to wish she hadn't made a slip she already regretted. Pasting on a smile, she looked up at him. "I decided three people living in the same mansion were too many, so I married Karl."

Nikos's expression darkened. "And you went to live in his castle where you discovered too late that without your money to keep it renovated, he wouldn't be able to provide you with a roof over your head." His fingers tightened. "Not exactly the match made in heaven you had in mind."

His rancor was too much. It filled her with fresh despair that the one person she'd thought she could turn to had only been a figment of her imagination before the veil had been removed from her eyes.

"You're right, so I'll keep looking."

His sculpted brows formed a black furrow across the bridge of his proud nose. "In all the wrong places. You have a proclivity for it."

The arrows kept hitting their mark. "I thought this was the right one. My mistake."

A glacial smile broke out on his striking face. "You're not apprehensive about being under *my* thumb?" he drawled silkily.

She glanced at his hand still gripping her arm.

No. His genuine kindness to Tracey in front of her grandfather had settled that concern years ago. Her mother had been a gentle woman whose approval of Nikos had only verified Tracey's own feelings that he could be trusted.

However, that had been before certain events had thrust her into the ugly spotlight of public opinion, destroying his ability to see her as anything but dross.

"You and I aren't family. Ours would be a business contract, not a marriage."

"There's little difference between them," he said in a cryptic tone before letting her go.

Without his touch, she felt strangely bereft.

"There's a world of difference when you're not

sharing a last name or a bed." She was looking beyond his shoulder to some guests who'd started toward Nikos, then recognized he was busy.

"My grandfather was very old world, Nikos, but you already know that. To him a woman belonged in the background to bear his children and cook his meals. Mother was an appendage.

"But I was born to a different father in a different time. I want to try my hand at the business."

"Of course you do." Following his hurtful mockery she heard a sharp intake of breath. "What is it you're really after, Tracey?"

"I've already told you. Guidance for six months. In that amount of time I know I could at least hold my own on the board, something mother didn't feel competent enough to do. I want to do it for her. But it appears that taking on a prince's discarded goods is too beneath you."

Bruise-like shadows appeared beneath his eyes. "Do you have any conception of what my help would entail?"

"You mean if you could see past my wild, wicked ways?" she baited him. "As a matter of fact, *no*. I came to Olympus to find that out from you. Naturally you would have to decide if you could spare the time *and* the risk of my being a quick study."

She lowered her eyes. "Should you want to get hold of me for any reason, I'll be at the Lagonissi Hotel in Athens until day after tomorrow."

"And then?"

The tension between them was palpable.

She flashed him a bright smile. "You're the all-seeing Helios. You tell me."

CHAPTER TWO

"I'LL GIVE YOU MY ANSWER NOW," came his swift response. "But not here. Let's go."

With a speed that had Tracey reeling, Nikos grasped her hand and fairly pulled her along toward the stairs leading down to the water. A tender stood by to ferry the guests to shore.

"I should at least say good-night to Mr. Padakis, and thank him." Tracey's grandfather had done business with the head of Padakis Shipping Lines. She had no desire to offend him.

"I'll phone him later and tell him an emergency arose."

Before she could countenance it, he'd helped her into a life jacket as if she were his little girl instead of a grown woman who'd existed without his help for twenty-five years.

The men on the party circuit never showed

concern for her welfare. It only took a few drinks before they were oblivious to anyone's needs. Not so Nikos, who was a different breed of man.

After giving a nod to one of the yacht staff, the boat skimmed the top of the calm water to the pier where he helped divest her of the preserver and assisted her up the steps to dry ground.

Through some invisible radar, a black limo with smoked windows appeared. He helped her in the back seat, then climbed in beside her and shut the door. Once out on the main road lined with paparazzi trying to get shots of the party, they sped away from the port, leaving the noise and glitter of the yacht behind.

She gave him a covert glance, drawn to the enigmatic man whose face and brilliance were known throughout the corporate world. He'd pulled out his cell phone to make several calls, speaking in low tones to someone in a volley of unintelligible Greek. After the last exchange, he hung up, extending his long, muscular legs.

Hardening herself against the power of his charisma, she came straight to the point. "Now that we're alone, what *is* your answer?"

In an instant Nikos's expression darkened like

a black thunderhead. "Paul wasn't one to waste time with preliminaries either. Beneath that misleading shell you're more like him than I realized."

It hurt to be compared to her grandfather, but Tracey couldn't let his observation deter her from her goal. Thrown by the unexpected barb when she was in turmoil waiting to hear his answer, she decided to change the subject, hoping to ease some of the tension.

"I've been a lot of places, but never to Greece."

He cocked his dark head. "Apparently the French Riviera is more your scene." By his derisory tone, Nikos wasn't about to let her forget her past for a second. "What do you think of my country so far?"

"From here, the landscape has a lonely beauty in the moonlight, doesn't it?"

His jaw hardened. "It's too soon since your mother's death to see anything for what it really is."

In other words, he'd looked beneath the surface and considered her too far gone to salvage.

Bitterly disappointed by his rejection, which she'd been dealing with for the last hour, she schooled her features not to react and stared blindly out the window.

"All my life I've been patronized by my grandfather. Somehow I expected you to be different."

"Touché."

The wounds he'd inflicted would never heal.

"Nikos—"

"I'm prepared to become your mentor," he cut her off almost angrily. "Is that direct enough for you?"

A shock wave of excitement passed through her body. Her fingers gripped the sides of her black evening bag in reaction. "I thought you were telling me something else."

"I was."

She bit her lip. "You mean that mourning distorts everything."

He darted her a speaking glance. "Ten years ago I recall meeting a girl who was still grieving for her father."

Her grandfather had warned her of Nikos's abilities. He saw more than she wanted him to see.

"Where are we going?"

"To my condo in Athens. I've phoned your hotel and asked them to bring your belongings over. My housekeeper's preparing your room as we speak."

The thought of sleeping under his roof gave

her a fluttery feeling inside. "You didn't have to do that."

"But you knew I would," came the caustic remark, deepening her wound with lethal precision. "When I first met you, I had no idea you would grow up to be so transparent, yet feel no shame for it."

A shudder passed through her body.

"However, I do owe your mother something for playing hostess to me when I came to the mansion. Until now, circumstances haven't allowed me to reciprocate."

"Then let me thank you for her," she whispered.

He ignored her comment.

Tracey was intelligent enough to know he wouldn't enter into any kind of contract without a clause that made the negotiation palatable to him.

She wouldn't have come to him empty-handed, but he'd already thrown the stock offer back in her face.

Therefore, he intended to extract something else from her, like a complete transformation from the sybaritic woman portrayed in the tabloids. In that regard she was way ahead of him.

"If you're worried about my behavior, don't be.

Once you give me a few pointers every day, I swear that's what I'll concentrate on to the exclusion of all else."

If he was listening, she couldn't tell.

"I want you to be able to carry on your business affairs as though I weren't there. Where it comes to your personal life, I promise not to interfere."

Still no comment from him.

"If you'd like, you can live at the mansion while you're helping me. You're welcome to pick out any number of the rooms to turn into temporary headquarters for your company."

"I have a distinct aversion to somber mausoleums."

Tracey couldn't have put it better herself. She'd always hated it, and couldn't bear the thought of entering it again, let alone living there, but Nikos would never believe her.

"Before Mother died, we talked about turning the mansion into the Loretto Center for Italian immigrants who need a place to live and eat while training for a job."

"Your mother's idea is brilliant."

It was Tracey's idea, but there was no point in

trying to convince him of anything. His mind was made up against her.

"The center will run on a perpetual fund, which will keep it going and support a staff." She rested her head against the back of the seat and closed her eyes. "With Mother gone, I'd prefer to move into something small and cozy."

"You mean a fifty-room villa in the South of France. I'm afraid I'm allergic to those, too."

"As beautiful as the Côte d'Azur is, I intend to make Buffalo my home again. There's a hotel near the office that will do just fine."

A sound of derision came from his throat. "Before forty-eight hours have passed, you'll be back with your party crowd," he prophesied with conviction.

"Try me and you'll find out I'm a hard worker. When I decide to do something, nothing deters me."

"That's true. And being the infamous Tracey Loretto, whatever you choose to do, your behavior scoops the headlines. You're the darling of the tabloids."

Stop, Nikos. You're killing me.

"For the next six months you won't see my

name or my picture in the media because I'll be in hiding while I work. I did it before, and I can do it again."

He cast her a disbelieving glance. Why was she wasting her breath?

While they'd been talking—correction—while she'd been talking and he'd been systematically destroying her with every comeback—the limo had pulled up in front of a modern-looking apartment building overlooking the Acropolis. This was where he spent the greater portion of his time when he wasn't traveling. She'd always wondered...

He got out of the back and came around to help her to the ground, a god from Olympus wearing a mortal's formal black evening clothes. Despite his hostility, his nearness affected her equilibrium, causing her to cling to his arm. It was a mistake. She felt a tingling sensation not unlike a current of electricity and sprang away from him.

"We're up so high," she cried softly. "It's spectacular."

"Lykavittos is the tallest hill in Athens. It's convenient to the city center near my office on Alexandras Avenue."

When he cupped her elbow to usher her inside

the elegant lobby, she was acutely aware of his touch. "From the penthouse you'll find the view even more breathtaking."

Nothing could be more breathtaking than Nikos himself.

She had a struggle to prevent her excitement at being with him from showing. There had been a moment on the yacht when she'd thought he would walk away from her for good.

Her grandfather had never allowed her the privilege of spending time alone with Nikos. Tracey decided she was glad. Tonight she'd been able to approach him with the element of surprise on her side.

Though her reputation preceded her, she knew she'd shocked him much more with her business proposal. Now she had to wait on tenterhooks to hear his terms.

He pulled out a remote to open the elevator door. While they rode the short distance to the top, he studied her with heart-stopping intensity.

"Did you know that every time your grandfather planned a trip to Athens, I issued the invitation for you and your mother to come with him?"

Her heart leaped.

"No." She looked away, afraid he'd seen the flare in her eyes and be aware of her reaction. "He never took us with him. Except for a few occasional visitors like you to the mansion, he kept us apart from his business. In his world, women and children were always relegated to the background."

"I noticed he had no women on his staff or his board."

"Some of the best CEOs are women," she asserted. "But you could never convince him of that. If my grandmother had feelings on the subject, she never expressed them to my mother or me."

She took another quick breath. "Nikos—I swear not to make your life hell. All I need is to absorb enough of your knowledge to become a viable member of the board. Hopefully I won't get in your way too much."

He darted her an enigmatic glance. Though it wasn't as openly judgmental as before, she still felt uncomfortable.

"I promise not to complicate your life any more than I can help. You have no idea how important this is to me."

How she longed to surprise her grandfather's chauvinistic colleagues. It was something she would relish almost as much as proving a female Loretto could get the job done.

"I think I do," came the oblique response.

To her relief the elevator door opened. She felt the blessed cool of the air-conditioning as he walked her through the entrance hall into a spacious living room. The understated elegance provided the perfect foil for the wall of glass overlooking the birthplace of civilization.

He opened one of the sliding doors for her to move out on the veranda. She gravitated to the railing. "Oh—how incredibly beautiful." The heat of the day was still rising from the streets.

"Helios warned that to look down upon Athens meant to be eternally enslaved."

She darted him a curious glance. "I don't recall having read that anywhere. Are you sure he said it?"

For the first time all night, the chiseled lines of his male mouth relaxed. "Are you sure he didn't? I thought you were the expert."

A teasing Nikos made him seem younger and took her back ten years to the first time she'd met him. Since then he'd grown even more attractive if that was possible. Certainly more than her senses could handle. Being here with him like this caused her to tremble at the enormity of what she'd done by asking for his help.

Was it possible he was like the all-knowing god Helios who'd seen past the bad behavior into the heart of a once lovestruck teen and read the truth there?

But she was grown up now, and had put romantic fantasies away. By the time she'd learned from him, he wouldn't be bothered by her again if he'd just give her the chance.

"I feel badly about taking you away from the party. I was hoping that if you would tell me exactly what you expect for helping me, then you could go back to the yacht and carry on with any business you were conducting."

"That's very thoughtful of you," came the mocking reply.

Not for the first time tonight did she find herself wondering why he sounded so embittered. Disgusted, turned off by the way the media had portrayed her maybe, but there had to be a deeper reason why every comment from him felt like a crushing blow.

"Whatever you insist on believing, I'm not giving lip service, Nikos."

He seemed to ponder her words. "When the waiter approached carrying your note, I'd been looking for a legitimate excuse to leave early. I daresay your business proposition is more intriguing than any I've encountered to date."

Tracey took another deep breath. "Asking you this favor is a drastic move. Perhaps too drastic. I'm afraid it was the only way I could think of to insulate myself against the board members and achieve results.

"In order not to be the laughing stock of the company, I need to do something that will ensure I don't fail. But considering how revolted you are by my lifestyle, coming to you with any expectations has taught me a lesson that no slap in the face could have achieved."

A bleakness entered his eyes before he bit out an epithet, making her more uneasy than ever. But she had to get this said.

"There are other successful businessmen even wealthier than you I could have approached and still can," she continued. "Not many, I agree, but a few. However, my first instinct was to get in contact with you.

"Despite certain obstacles and the disparity in our ages, I felt you were a friend." She cast him another searching glance. "By the time the six months are up, I hope you'll come to think of me as one, too."

His black brows knit together. "The most important thing you need to learn about running a company is to go with your first instinct, which comes straight from the gut. Never second-guess yourself."

She moistened her dry lips. "That would be fine, except that I'm still waiting for you to tell me what you want out of this arrangement, since it's not money."

His eyes grew shuttered. "Are you willing to wait a little longer and see…"

Uh-oh. She folded her arms in an effort to stop the shivers from traveling over her body.

Nikos wasn't like other men. He didn't do things the way ordinary mortals did them. That's what had put the fear in her grandfather.

There was no question she would say yes.

Once she did, she would be committed—an

oath sworn never to be broken. This was the gospel according to Nikos Lazaridis. It terrified and excited her all at the same time.

"Yes," she declared.

His golden eyes impaled her. "Be very sure."

"I'm sure." The thought of returning to the emptiness of her life left by her mother's death was too much for Tracey to contemplate. "So sure in fact that I have another favor to ask."

"Go ahead," he muttered.

"Do you have a problem with us getting to work right away? I realize you have your own business affairs to run. But if you could see your way clear to start me on something, anything— I'd be grateful."

She spied an odd glimmer of satisfaction in his eyes, as if he were complimenting her for thinking like a businesswoman. "I'd prefer it."

"Good. I'm anxious to dig in."

"Will tomorrow be soon enough for you?"

"You're willing to fly back to Buffalo with me that fast?"

After a slight pause, he said, "We'll talk about it over lunch."

Tracey still had a hard time believing she was

here in Greece with the man who, like a distant star system, had always been out of reach. "What time would you like me to be ready?"

His hooded gaze swept over her features. "Noon. Judging by those shadows under your eyes, you're exhausted and need the rest."

"Rest? What's that?"

"Indeed."

With that one word she felt his disdain for an empty life that was all party and little sleep. He had no way of knowing that for two months she hadn't budged from her mother's bedside. Watching her die had drained Tracey until she was emotionally spent.

"The guest bedroom is the first door on your right down the hall. If you're hungry I'll ask my housekeeper to make up a tray for you."

"I ate at the party, but thank you all the same."

He nodded. "If there's anything you need during the night, just tell me. My room is right across from yours. While you're under my roof, everything I have is yours."

Just like that? After his debilitating repudiation of her, she couldn't credit the benign change in him.

Suddenly she worried she didn't know him at all. Yet she'd been the one to approach him.

It all came down to *trust*.

Without it, there was no point to anything.

He studied her dispassionately. "Are you having second thoughts?"

"For your sake, yes," she declared. "I've asked something of you unprecedented in anyone's book." She cleared her throat. "A simple thank you hardly covers my gratitude."

His gaze shone a glittery gold as it wandered over her features, filling her body with unexpected warmth. "One day you'll learn I never undertake anything unless it's what I want. Good night, Tracey. Sleep well."

She eyed him soulfully. "Does Helios ever sleep? I wonder," she murmured before going inside.

Nikos watched her voluptuous figure disappear from the living room. She'd come to him out of the velvety darkness with a supposed "strictly business" proposition. But he knew why she'd really shown up. She was hoping for a marriage proposal out of him.

He noticed she'd gone to bed across the hall

from his bedroom without the pretense of a modest demur. That was because she expected a visit from him in the wee small hours, at which time they would make love. She assumed he would be so desirous of her body, he would tell her they were getting married, forget the phony ploy she'd used to get his attention on the yacht. Then she would gloat over her triumph in becoming Mrs. Nikos Lazaridis.

A cold smile broke out on his dark features.

Her sleep would remain undisturbed. She would need all the rest she could get in order to deal with the shock that awaited her tomorrow.

Without wasting any time he went to his study to make some phone calls, forgetting that he'd left a certain newspaper sitting on his desk. Helpless to do otherwise, his gaze fell on the week-old headlines.

Diana Loretto, only daughter of deceased millionaire Mustard King Paul Loretto, died last night at their Italianate mansion in Buffalo, New York, of cancer. She leaves her only daughter, Tracey Von Axel, who is now heiress to the Loretto fortune.

The partying ex-wife of playboy Prince Karl Von Axel of Luxembourg couldn't be found for comment. Rumor has it the beautiful, enormously wealthy redheaded granddaughter of Paul Loretto was dancing the night away in Monaco with a coterie of jet-set boyfriends when she heard the news.

Feeling once again as if he'd been impaled by a battering ram, Nikos Lazaridis tossed the copy of the *H Naytemiiopikh* in the waste basket. Normally the Greek business newspaper he read every morning didn't deal with tabloid sensationalism. But news of that magnitude had made headlines everywhere.

When a twenty-five-year-old hedonistic heiress who'd never done a day's work in her life, and didn't know the meaning of the word *monogamy*, was suddenly thrust to the helm of a male-dominated blue-chip company, the stock market would be affected.

What a waste of a life! Where had the innocent girl he knew gone?

Years ago when he'd first met her, he'd thought...

His hands slowly formed into fists. Damn. It didn't matter what he'd thought.

"Simon?" he spoke to his assistant the second he'd gotten him on the phone.

"Yes, Nikos?"

"I've had a change in plans and won't be coming into the office for a while. You're in charge. I'll let you know the rest of my agenda later."

His next call was to Giorgios Padakis. After explaining why they'd left the party early, Nikos invited him and his wife to have lunch with them at his favorite restaurant in the Plaka tomorrow.

Once it was arranged, he called his brother's house in Kalambaka.

"Nikos?" he answered after being called to the phone.

"*Yasoo*, Leon."

"I thought you were partying on the Padakis yacht tonight." No doubt the affair had been covered on the evening news.

"I left early," he explained. "Tell me something. Are you still uninterested in the old farmhouse?"

"That pile of rubble? It's an eyesore."

Nikos had been hoping for that response.

"What about the few acres it sits on, if only for sentimental value?"

"Papa killed himself working that soil to death. I never liked farming and have no desire to hold onto it. If you've found a buyer, sell it. How much is he offering?"

"Three times its worth on today's market." Nikos would have said a hundred times, but knew his brother's pride wouldn't be able to handle Nikos paying him ten million Euros for it. He could hear Leon's mind turning things over.

"Why would he do that unless he's discovered oil this far from the Sahara—"

Nikos was used to Leon's sarcasm and his brother hadn't disappointed him. "Not oil. Something better."

A brusque laugh came from the other end of the phone. "Who in the hell wants it? Let alone enough to overpay?"

"*I* do," Nikos said in a quiet voice. He'd always wanted it.

His brother cursed under his breath.

Leon didn't want the farm, and had refused it outright for years. But he didn't want Nikos to have it. Since their father's death they'd both gone their own ways and didn't talk about the painful past.

The eventual fire that had destroyed part of the vacated structure seemed to have signaled the end of Nikos's sense of family togetherness as surely as the small tract of land left to go fallow. But Tracey's unexpected intrusion had provided the catalyst to put certain plans he'd been considering for some time into motion.

"I'll have the bank do an electronic funds transfer to your account in the morning, Leon. In case you see activity going on at the farmhouse tomorrow, don't be alarmed. Some workmen will be out to turn on the water and electricity."

In fact by tomorrow night a whole cleaning crew would have been needed to perform a minor miracle in order to make the usable rooms bearable to live in. He'd need part of the night to make the necessary phone calls for services and provisions.

"I'll talk to you soon." Nikos hung up before his brother could tell him he'd changed his mind about selling. The die was cast. There was no going back, not for him or Tracey.

By her own words, she'd signed her death sentence.

The shorn little mermaid whose infamous behavior produced millions of dollars for the gutter press would stay landlocked away from her would-be lovers in the heart of the Thessaly plain.

CHAPTER THREE

TRACEY FOUND THE RESTAURANT Daphne's to be a beautiful town-house taverna in the Plaka with Pompei-style murals decorating the main dining room. To her surprise Giorgios Padakis and his wife, Stella, were waiting for them.

After Nikos explained that he'd invited them because Giorgios had done business with her grandfather and she could benefit from that association, they were shown to a table.

Before there was any mention of business, Nikos talked her into trusting him to order for her. He insisted that the veal braised with quince was the best Tracey would ever eat.

One taste of the sumptuous appetizer of grilled lamb with light yogurt and mint brought to the table and she believed him.

"This meal is a masterpiece. I'm glad you

brought me here," she said later, after the dessert had been served. "No wonder my grandfather loved coming to Athens."

"Actually Paul preferred Italian food. He never ate here."

That sounded like her intransigent grandfather. "Then he missed out."

Giorgios eyed her from across the table. "I must admit I'm surprised he didn't groom you to take a seat on the board. You were wise to approach Nikos for help. When you're ready, I'll be happy to explain where I fit into the mosaic of your family's business."

"Thank you, Mr. Padakis."

"Call me Giorgios."

"All right, Giorgios. I will."

Stella patted her hand. "I'm very proud of you, Tracey. You make me want to be young again and do something truly worthwhile."

Tracey shook her head. "We'll see about the worthwhile part. But if I don't make the grade, you can be sure it won't be Nikos's fault."

"You won't fail," Giorgios declared. "Your grandfather did remarkable things with the company. Since his death, some people have lost

confidence. But when you spring on the scene—"
He spread his arms wide. "Who knows where his
granddaughter will take it in the next decade?"

"Hopefully not to pot," Tracey quipped.

A burst of laughter came from Giorgios.

Not so Nikos, who reached over with the intention of pouring her some wine, increasing her
awareness of his potent masculinity.

She put her hand over the goblet. "None for
me. I got sick on my first glass of champagne
years ago and haven't touched alcohol since."

He flashed her a puzzled glance, which was
mirrored in the others' faces, too. The tabloids
would have people believe she'd been on a con-
tinuous drunken binge for years. Nikos didn't
trust anything she said. It took every bit of re-
straint not to beg him to believe her.

With his fabulous dark looks and the expensive
silk suit of pale blue fitting his well-honed body
like a glove, she found it difficult to breathe.
There wasn't a woman in sight who hadn't
singled him out.

When she looked away she noticed Giorgios
studying her while he munched on the last of his
figs topped in ouzo and cream sauce. "Forgive

me for staring at you throughout our meal, my dear, but you have the rare coloring of a Titian painting."

"I was thinking the same thing," his wife, Stella, commented, "especially in that dress."

Nikos nodded. "Before we left the condo I told her it was the ideal accompaniment to her hair."

Tracey still felt light-headed from his appraisal. It had traveled slowly over the filmy, oyster-toned dress that draped the mold of her curving body.

"Thank you for your kind words. I'm afraid my grandfather thought red hair obscene."

"Surely he was joking!" Stella remarked.

"My father had red hair. Let's just say he and my grandfather had a history of clashing."

She thought Nikos grimaced before standing up from the table. He put his hands on her chair to help her. His fingers grazed the back of her neck, sending little sensations of delight coursing through her nervous system.

"I hate to bring this to a close, but we have much to accomplish before this day is over. You two stay and enjoy another cup of coffee."

"Thank you for joining us," Tracey inserted. "After that fabulous party on the yacht last night,

I don't know how you have the energy for anything else. No wonder my grandfather spoke so highly of you."

Giorgios got to his feet. "Be assured I'm at your service any time you need it, Tracey."

"I appreciate that more than you know."

The older couple couldn't have been nicer. Despite their bad opinion of her, good manners kept them from treating her the way Nikos had done on the yacht last night.

She smiled at both of them, then Nikos cupped her elbow and ushered her through the tables to the front entrance. He was anxious to leave. She could feel his energy.

On their way out to the limo parked along the street, they had to run a gauntlet of paparazzi hanging around for photo opportunities. They flung humiliating, degrading questions at her. Tonight it would be on the news that she'd deserted Prince Karl for Mr. Lazaridis.

Much as she would love to defend herself and tell the truth about a lot of things that would make the lies about her seem tame in comparison, she couldn't.

Tracey turned her head away from the men

running alongside them with their cameras, and met Nikos's penetrating stare. It seemed to say all the things he'd thrown at her last evening. For a little while in the restaurant she'd forgotten. She hated it when he looked at her like that.

"I'm sorry, Nikos," she murmured after they'd gotten in the limo.

"About what?"

"That you have to be seen with me."

"It's a little late for regrets."

"I know, but I *am* concerned for you. Whatever woman you've been seeing lately is going to be hurt to discover you were out in public with me."

Tracey could appreciate that any woman hoping to maintain a close relationship with a man like Nikos would be devastated to see him on the ten o'clock news in the company of that Loretto woman.

"She'll live."

So there was someone…

"Will she? How do you know she's not in love with you, and seeing you with me will break her heart?"

Maybe it was a trick of light, but she thought she glimpsed a brief look of incredulity, even pain in Nikos's eyes. No. She had to have been mistaken about the pain.

"Honestly, Nikos, I'm used to the dreadful things people say about me. Under the circumstances it's your girlfriend who will have to be very understanding. In that department I'm afraid you're the one who'd be taking all the risks."

"Risks are what I thrive on." He lounged back, making her aware of his powerful physique. "But it's true that no matter what you and I know and understand between ourselves, we can't run from the fact that the world will view us as a man and woman living together for the usual reasons. Giorgios is a case in point."

"Whatever he believes about me, at least he kept it to himself." She took a fortifying breath. "Thank you for lunch. I was glad to spend some time with him and his wife. They're decent, generous people."

"He couldn't take his eyes off you."

A tight band seemed to constrict her lungs. "I'll always be the scarlet woman to you, won't I? If you intend to keep reminding me of my past, it's going to make our working relationship difficult."

"Giorgios believes you're my mistress. He envies me."

"Since you already have one, I can't think why you would say that except to remind me of my own flaws. Could we please talk about something else?"

His eyes were veiled as he said, "Are you up for a helicopter ride?"

Evidently they were leaving for the airport. "Why do you ask?"

"I don't know all your secret fears."

That sounded like the Nikos she'd idolized from day one. The man who showed a constant concern for her welfare, as if her wishes were important to him.

She bowed her head. "You think I have a lot of them?"

"What matters is that I know the one that brought you to me." It certainly had done that. "I'm still waiting for an answer. Do we take the helicopter or not? I recall a time in front of your grandfather when you said you were terrified of them."

"My mother was afraid to fly, period. I pretended to be afraid too, so I wouldn't have to be alone with him."

Her answer must have disturbed Nikos on some level because his expression closed up. Wherever he was taking them, she sensed he was in a hurry.

"You won't tell me where we're going?"

"I'd prefer to surprise you."

With that answer, she had to be content.

Knowing Nikos, she imagined he'd taken the day off from his busy schedule to secret them away to a private place in order to work out their plans for the next six months.

During the drive to the heliport, she had to keep reminding herself this was a purely business arrangement. Try telling her heart that. It kept running away with her. She was still in this feverish state when they climbed in his helicopter and took off in a hot, cloudless sky.

One look at Nikos, who sat opposite the pilot, looking more splendid than any male mortal, she could believe they were headed for the resting place of the gods.

The sight of a golden afternoon sun blazing down on the bustling metropolis of Athens formed a dazzling picture she would always associate with Greece. The pilot treated her to a mini tour over the ancient city with its magnificent Parthenon.

Eventually the landscape changed.

According to Nikos they were flying northwest toward his birthplace in Kalambaka, Greece. To hear him talk about his beginnings and point out landmarks in a voice that couldn't hide his excitement, gave her new insight into his psyche.

En route he mesmerized her with his knowledge of the land once claimed by Macedonians, Romans and the Ottoman Turks. Caught up in past lore, she cried out with surprised delight when the vista opened up to a great sweeping plain of lush green with the snow-capped mounts of Pelion and Parnassus in the far distance.

The pilot took them down low. After following the Pinios River, they flew over carpets of red poppies interspersed with yellow mustard crops forming a gigantic patchwork of colors.

Riveted to such indescribable beauty, she wasn't prepared for the sight that awaited her when the helicopter came face-to-face with fantastic, gigantic spires of gray rock. They jutted at least four hundred feet from the fertile valley floor in the strangest shapes imaginable.

"Oh Nikos!" Her fingers dug into the armrests as the helicopter rose higher and higher to escape crashing into them.

The man at the controls chuckled. "Behold the Meteora, Ms. Loretto."

Tracey had seen them in a James Bond film, but not even the movie could have prepared her for this experience. The pilot was like a magician, allowing them to hover at the top while her eyes fastened on the ancient monasteries clinging to the cliffs.

"Not exactly the kind of spot you normally frequent," Nikos said in a cool aside.

This was the second time in an hour he'd alluded to her reckless past. Somehow she was going to have to grow a second skin that wouldn't allow his painful remarks to penetrate. She'd agreed to wait and see what it was he wanted from her. But if he kept this up…

Before she could think of something to say that might soften him, they veered toward the town of Kalambaka with its clusters of red-orange roofed houses nestled in the valley beyond the rocks. Her heart pounded with growing momentum to realize this whole area had been his backyard as a boy.

Her confusion began when the pilot headed

toward a spot beyond the town, and set them down in the middle of a barren field.

A little way off stood a deserted-looking one-story stone farmhouse. She could tell fire had destroyed the rear portion of the rectangular structure a long time ago. Her gaze darted to a white truck loaded with items. It was parked outside on the dirt track leading in from the road.

Before Tracey could ask if there'd been a malfunction of the helicopter and that's why they landed, Nikos was on his feet, lowering their luggage to the ground. He urged her to undo her seat belt, then helped her climb out while the rotors were still turning.

Evidently this stop had been planned. When Nikos had promised there would be no journalists around to invade their privacy, he'd really meant it!

At the last second she remembered her manners and called out her thanks to the pilot, who appeared ready to take off again. By this time Nikos had moved their two suitcases out of the way in one effortless male gesture. The two men waved to each other before the helicopter rose in the air, quickly gaining altitude.

Without giving a hint of what he was about to do next, Nikos unexpectedly turned and picked her up in his arms. He was so strong, her head fell helplessly against his broad chest where she could feel his heart pounding.

"Nikos?" Her cheeks went hot. "What are you doing? If you're planning to drive us into town, you don't need to worry about my shoes getting dirty. The truck's only a few yards away."

His expression remained unreadable, as if he hadn't heard her. "We're standing on ground belonging to my family for over a hundred years." He started toward the front door with her.

This humble dwelling had produced one of the most remarkable men in all Greece?

The moment was surreal. She could hardly find the words.

"How long did you live here?"

"Seventeen years."

He put a key in the lock and opened it. "You're about to cross over the threshold of the home where my mother gave birth to me."

The words came out muffled because he'd spoken with his face buried in her silky red hair. He was almost crushing her, but she realized his emotions had gripped him so hard, he wasn't aware of it.

After carrying her inside, he flipped on a switch that illuminated a single lightbulb hanging from the ceiling without a fixture. She imagined this had been a living room, but it was devoid of any furnishings. Old linoleum whose color had faded with age covered the floors.

"When was the last time you were here?" she whispered.

"A week after my father passed away from a bad liver, I left for Athens to find work, and haven't stepped inside since."

"Nikos—" she said, her voice throbbing. "The memories must be overpowering."

"Yes." He slowly put her down, sounding far away from her right then. "My mother died on the couch in this room."

Still in mourning over the loss of her own mother, Tracey staggered with grief. "How agonizing for you. Why did she die so young?"

"An infection."

Tracey thought he was about to say something else, then thought the better of it. It was impossible to swallow. "How old were you?"

"Twelve. Leon was fourteen."

"Leon?" she questioned.

"My brother."

"I didn't realize you had a sibling. You've never talked about him. Grandfather never said anything."

"I only told Paul what I wanted him to know."

She could understand that better than anyone. "Where does your brother live?"

"In Kalambaka with his wife and two children. He despised anything to do with farming and moved into town at the same time I left the farm."

That had to have been a lonely experience. His parents gone, no brother to go away with him.

Her eyes closed tightly. She could relate, feeling herself overwhelmed by those same emotions.

"Do you see each other often?"

"When time permits," he ground out. She bit her lip, sensing another source of tension coming from him. "Now that we're here, he'll be dropping by to satisfy his curiosity."

Dropping by *where* exactly?

"Come with me. I'll show you the rest."

End of subject.

The smell of cleaning products filled her

nostrils. The heat of the day within these walls stifled her, making the odors even stronger. Someone had been in here earlier scrubbing everything down.

They passed through the open partition into a kitchen-cum-dining area. With no stick of furniture and small windows, everything looked forlorn beneath another single lightbulb. But slices of his former life had to be bombarding him like splinters of crystal flung in his direction.

If this were her home, she'd be too overcome with poignant memories to function. How did he manage to carry on?

Beyond the kitchen there was a narrow hallway. One side of it was boarded up. "The bedrooms?" she queried.

He gave her a sober nod. "For the most part they've been destroyed, so we had them sealed off."

"How did the fire start?"

"Vandals most likely. It's a miracle the whole place didn't burn to the ground. When Leon called me about it, we decided someone must have come along and frightened them off before they could finish the job."

Another door led to a covered back porch.

Behind the last door in the hall was a bathroom with a tub, sink and mirror, nothing else. Nikos flushed the toilet and turned on one of the faucets. "We have hot water."

Her body quickened.

The premonition that he planned for them to live here caused the hairs to prickle on the back of her neck.

Now that we're here, my brother will be dropping by.

The golden eyes that flicked to hers were banked by a mysterious glow.

When she'd told Nikos she would prefer a cozy place rather than stay in her family's Italianate mansion, she'd had no idea what was in his mind.

It wasn't as if staying here was beneath her. Far from it. This had been his family home, and as such was precious to her, too.

She was simply having difficulty imagining how they were going to accomplish her business from Greece, let alone from inside these bare white walls that had sustained years of neglect.

"This farmhouse isn't quite as primitive as the barn your Loretto ancestor slept in when he emigrated to America in 1873. But a farm is still a farm, and the same process will be in effect."

Alarmed she said, "What are you trying to tell me?"

"We won't be working in New York," he announced with an underlying note of finality.

"I've gathered that much, but I still don't understand."

"An office is a place to shove paper around. If you want to know what makes Loretto's tick, you need to begin at the grassroots." His eyes pierced hers. "I'm going to turn you into a farmer."

A farmer?

But not even grass grew here!

"Without the farmer, there'd be no Loretto's. So we'll live here. You'll work the land, do the accounts, make the necessary purchases out of your budget just like your ancestor Emilio Loretto did. You'll be walking in his shoes, so to speak."

Weakness attacked her body.

"I—I've heard his name of course," she stammered, "but don't know much about him from grandfather except that he was a great businessman."

"He was a great deal more than that," Nikos

declared. "Emilio, fresh off the boat from Italy with only five hundred lire sewn in the lining of his coat, found shelter in a barn and worked on the owner's farm. His wages were paid out in tomatoes and mustard seeds, which he began selling door-to-door.

"Eventually he moved to a rooming house where he bottled the vegetables, then peddled them in the city. After experimenting with oil, vinegar and ground mustard, he discovered that the combination emulsified and made a tasty salad dressing, which he marketed. The result became a household name."

"How did you know all that?" Tracey was dumbfounded.

"I make it a habit to learn everything possible about the people I do business with. I start with their beginnings, which tell me how hungry they are to be successful."

"What did you learn about my grandfather?"

"That nothing less than a prince was good enough for his granddaughter."

Tracey shivered. Nikos understood a lot, but not everything.

"In time you'll learn what you need to know

to sit on your grandfather's board and make judicious decisions," he continued to speak. "Your practical knowledge will give you that needed edge. I'll help you.

"Just pretend you're fresh off the boat and ready to stake your claim in the New World."

Tracey gulped.

New World was right.

The New World within the Old, presenting an oxymoron of precarious ramifications. She knew it would take blood, sweat, tears, a backhoe, a tractor and heaven knew what else. And that was only for the outside of the farmhouse!

She stared back at him, hugging her arms to her waist. "I don't think I can do this."

Nikos darted her a sardonic smile. "I'm sure my mother said the same thing when she married my father and he brought her out here to farm. Her parents were shopkeepers in Larissa. Though she didn't resemble you in any way, shape or form, she was a city girl, too."

You got yourself into this, Tracey Loretto.

She'd sought Nikos's expertise. By asking for his help, she had no right to question his methods now.

"I can see bringing you here has come as a shock. But with time, patience and a little back-breaking work, this land will produce a good mustard crop for you. The kind your ancestor helped cultivate in New York for the owner, and eventually for himself.

"Without hands-on experience to understand the beginnings of your family's business, how can you hope to make informed suggestions for its future? Loretto's started with the farmer. From there, everything else sprang into existence. But never forget the farmer keeps it going. Without him, the company fails."

His wisdom shouldn't have astounded her, but it did. Good heavens—now she knew why Nikos's reputation preceded him. The man was a genius.

Her fingers tightened around her handbag. "You really think I could do it?"

"You're a Loretto, aren't you?" He eyed her shrewdly. "But until you try, you won't know if you'll be successful. That all depends on whether you have fire in the belly."

In other words, did she have the guts to see this through long enough to find out? Finally she had the answer to his "wait and see" proposition.

More than ever she stood in awe of Nikos, who'd been a farmer first and knew how to sift the proverbial chaff from the wheat.

He was convinced the supposedly spoiled rotten, amoral, good-for-nothing heiress he despised would be gone by morning, no longer wasting his time. By putting her to the ultimate test, he would be rid of her once and for all.

Tracey moved over to one of the newly cleaned windows and looked out on a field that had lain unproductive for twenty-one years. In her mind's eye she could see the lush crops of mustard and poppy flowers they'd flown over earlier.

How clever of him to show her a vision of what it could look like with time and hard work, knowing she could never rise to the occasion. She had an idea he was waiting for her to round on him and demand he take her back to civilization.

Nikos came to stand behind her. "How do you like my country now?" The insidious question wrapped in velvet worked its way into her consciousness.

There was a gallantry in Nikos that wouldn't have allowed him to refuse her initial request.

Instead he'd used his common sense and wits to make her face reality.

Wouldn't he love for her to say "Yes, it's asking too much of me." Then he'd be legitimately rid of her and she'd have no one to blame but herself. But she'd come too far to back down. Never mind that the thought of not being around him all the time sounded quite unbearable to her already.

Her glance wandered to the truck parked outside. The contents behind the cab were no longer a mystery. Nikos was one person who planned for every contingency. That was what made him unique among men.

If she was ready to thrust in the sickle, then he was, too. If she decided the task before her was too huge, he'd provided her with an escape route, giving her the means to drive away and not look back.

Straightening her shoulders, she turned around with a smile, her eyes seeking his. "The sun has dropped below the horizon. I'd say we have a lot to do before dark to make our farmhouse habitable. After I get my suitcase, I'll change so I can help you unload."

He held her glance for an overly long moment. Disbelief was etched in every unforgettable male feature.

Was he giving her a final chance to recall her words? She had an idea Nikos wasn't surprised about anything very often, but twice in twenty-four hours she seemed to have caught him off guard.

As she started for the living room, he grasped her arm, holding her back. The contact shot fire through her body.

"The ground is unforgiving. In those high heels you could twist an ankle, but I'm not giving you the chance for that to happen. You've got a crop to put in, so stay where you are," he thundered in a tone that brooked no argument.

Quickly letting go of her, Nikos strode through the house.

That was why he'd carried her in from the helicopter? So she couldn't pull a female ploy that would result in her being unable to get to work right away? Was every move he made dictated by an agenda?

She could well understand why her grandfather had been frightened of him.

On legs that were still trembling from his

touch, Tracey disobeyed his edict and hurried over to the opposite window to watch him get their bags.

She pressed her forehead against the glass. He could have found them another unworked farm anywhere else. So what had driven him to bring her to his birthplace where they'd have to start from scratch on every front, not just the land?

He'd revealed enough emotion to make her realize he was battling some demons from his past. Tracey understood. On that score it seemed she and Nikos had something in common.

He brought their suitcases in first. Afraid to look at him in this mood, she reached for hers and disappeared into the bathroom. After removing her dress, she quickly changed into some white pleated pants and a cotton navy top with small white swirls. These clothes were too dressy for housework, let alone farming, but she hadn't come equipped with overalls.

After slipping on sandals, she emerged to help him. Nikos worked fast. He'd already brought in two camp cots and bedding, two folding chairs and a folding camp table.

Tracey hurried outside after him. Nikos's

back was turned to her. All that was left were some boxes to bring in. "This will be like camping out. I've never done it. Let me carry something."

She could feel his negative tension as he handed her a medium-sized one. This close she noticed he'd removed his suit jacket and tie. His white shirtsleeves had been rolled up to the elbow, displaying hard-muscled arms. He'd unbuttoned his shirt and pulled it from the waistband of his trousers.

Unable to do anything else, she stared at his solid masculine silhouette in the dying light. It didn't matter what he wore, or didn't. Nikos took her breath.

Afraid he would catch her looking, she turned away and went back inside the farmhouse. Once she'd put the box down, she started outside for another one. They worked in harmony. Before long everything had been unloaded from the truck.

His enigmatic gaze swept over her, sending a different kind of heat spiraling through her body. "Tomorrow morning we'll drive into town and buy some work clothes."

"Can we afford it?" she quipped, hoping to

lighten his truculent mood. "According to you, my ancestor didn't have enough money to buy anything."

"We might not have much more. I rarely carry large sums of money on me."

If he thought that put fear in her, then he was mistaken.

"Neither do I," she informed him with secret delight. "I'm afraid I parted with most of mine when I bribed the waiter."

His scowl prompted her to give an elegant shrug.

"Maybe we won't be going into town after all. Let's hope the truck still has some gas in it," she added, "or we might not be going anywhere. Maybe we'd better empty our pockets to see what we've got and make out a budget."

"I'm surprised you've heard of the word," he muttered.

"I learned a few things in college."

"What college? You got married and have been on a wild junket ever since."

Deciding to risk it, she said, "Even so, I managed to get an undergraduate degree and an MBA."

He flashed her a cruel smile. "Of course you did."

His derision was the one thing she had no defense against.

"I know you don't believe me. It was one of my best kept secrets from grandfather."

His eyes stared hard at her. "Where was this supposedly accomplished?"

"If you're ever curious enough to learn the truth, all you have to do is call the campus office at Schiller International University in Paris. Ask them if a Celine Calvet was a student there. I wore a short brown wig to remain incognito.

"Karl arranged it so word wouldn't get back to my grandfather. My ex-husband benefited from my money, and I benefited from Karl's title. Tit for tat."

Nikos went as still as a piece of petrified wood.

CHAPTER FOUR

"I PAID THE TUITION FEES OUT of the money my father put away for my schooling Grandfather didn't know about. To conserve my money, I lived, basically, out of a hotel."

"The George V you mean."

"No!" Tracey protested. "It was a little two-star close to the campus. I worked hard. It was during the summers and in between semesters that I went on those wild shopping binges and endless parties with or without my husband.

"Mostly without," she added at the last to bait Nikos because he seemed to thrive on it. "I found out that's the best way to do it. While you still have your wedding ring on your finger, nothing you say or do can be written in cement."

His lips tightened to a thin line. "Just in the tabloids."

He'd driven her over the edge.

"Do you know I'd have to count on more than these ten fingers how many marriage proposals have come my way from ambassadors, dukes, presidents, counts, earls, sheikhs, kings? All of whom have begged me to divorce Karl so they can get their greedy, grasping hands on my body and my money."

She flung her head back. "Wouldn't they be upset to believe however erroneously I came to Athens to snag myself a Greek god? It's a title none of them can lay claim to."

Tracey thought he'd gone a little paler around the lips. "So you're telling me that for the duration of your marriage, you've been living a double life."

"Yes!" Color steamed into her cheeks, the fallout from red hair. "I didn't care what people said. Talk is cheap. I was after something much more important. Karl kept the press busy while I went undercover every few months. It prevented grandfather from finding out what I was really doing behind his back."

His face had become a mask. He didn't know whether to believe her or not. At least she'd made a slight dent in that impenetrable armor.

Eyeing the furniture she said, "Shall we sleep in the living room?"

To her chagrin he gave her a contemptuous smile. "Reneging on your conditions already?"

"On these cots?"

Without waiting for him, she reached for one of the folded, lightweight beds and placed it against the wall to the left of the front door.

After undoing the hinge, it opened like a hospital cot. She spread it flat. Nikos followed with the bedding. Together they made it up.

While she put the pillow in the pillowcase, he picked up the other bed and placed it along the wall opposite the door. Before she could move to help him, he'd put on the sheet and blanket. She took care of the other pillow and tossed it to him.

Who would have dreamed he would bring her to a real farm to teach her boardroom business?

"These don't make bad couches." But she'd spoken too soon. The moment she plunked herself down, it started to give. If he hadn't come to the rescue and pulled her to her feet, she would have tipped to the floor.

Her body landed against his solid frame. The impact forced her to stay there for a fraction of a moment longer than was prudent, sending a thrill through her. He thrust her away, but not before she'd sensed his heart thudding against hers. With his chest exposed, there was only the thin layer of her top separating their skin.

"Next time I'll remember to distribute my weight more carefully," she murmured.

He turned from her and took the table and chairs into the dining room. She helped him set everything up in the middle of the floor beneath the light globe.

Darting him a furtive glance, she said, "I think my ancestor would probably have preferred sleeping on the hay to taking a chance with that cot."

An unbidden picture of Nikos inviting her to sleep in that barn with him filled her mind. While she could control her actions, it appeared she had no power over her thoughts, which were going to get her into serious trouble if she wasn't careful.

Needing to keep busy, she picked up his jacket and tie from the floor and draped them over one of the chairs. "You do wonder how Emilio fared," she mused aloud.

"You mean after he stepped off the boat thirsty and hungry?" Nikos could read her mind.

Their eyes met. "I thought you'd never get around to the subject."

The first glimmer of a truce shone from his eyes. "Our sea rations are in one of the boxes around here somewhere."

"Well, that gives me incentive to get everything unpacked in a hurry."

By the time she'd come across a box containing bottled water—joy!—she'd emptied half a dozen others. Nikos had done the same. The counter was now filled with bath towels, toilet paper, kitchen towels, soap, a small set of dishes, glasses, a set of cooking and eating utensils, a couple of saucepans and an electric fan.

"Heaven!" she cried when she saw it.

Nikos lifted it from the box and plugged it into a kitchen outlet. Within seconds they were drinking warm water in front of a balmy breeze blowing the suffocating air around.

Both of them soaked in perspiration, they'd turned into earthy creatures. Damp whorls of his thick black hair, which had a tendency to curl, clung to his neck. The lower half of his face and jaw had broken out in what she would call a nine o'clock shadow. His body gave off the last lingering trace of the soap he'd used, plus his own compelling male scent.

The sophisticated businessman, always impeccably dressed and groomed, was hidden away for the moment. Standing in front of her was an incredibly desirable Greek man of the soil, at home in surroundings that had nurtured him from the cradle.

Stripped of the outer trappings of the corporate world that had to weigh heavily at times, Tracey decided she liked him much better this way. The layers had been pealed away to reveal a set of broad shoulders and a well-defined chest with its dusting of black hair.

Exposed like a statue of Adonis, Nikos was much more beautiful. He was a living, breathing man who exuded a raw masculine appeal in every cut line and angle of his powerful physique. On top of everything else, nature had given him molten gold eyes and skin. No other embellishment was needed.

Caught feasting her eyes on him again, she

turned aside and put her empty water bottle on the kitchen counter. "That tasted good."

"Now for the pièce de résistance."

"I can't wait!"

"It's not sushi or pâté de foie gras," his voice rasped.

She eyed him with defiance. "I hate them both."

Another lie? she could hear him asking. A pause ensued before he handed her a roll and an orange from the last box.

"This is what I call a king's feast!" At this point she didn't care if he believed her or not.

For the next few minutes silence reigned while they stood there eating their fill. No bread or fruit had ever tasted so good before. Without refrigeration, nothing else would have been edible. But she wasn't thinking of that.

This moment was one of many forbidden fantasies she'd woven around Nikos during her teenage years. One in particular where she was alone with him on a picnic away from other people and the cares of the world.

He lay on a quilt while she leaned over him, feeding him grapes between kisses that kept growing longer and bolder until he didn't want food anymore. Only her…

"Here's a plum if you want it."

"Maybe later, but thank you." Breathless from her dangerous, unruly thoughts, she gathered up the peelings and put them in the empty orange bag. Then she washed her hands in the sink.

"While I take the boxes out to the truck, why don't you shower."

Was that a plea because she looked a complete mess? An imp got into her. "Wouldn't that be cheating?"

When she looked at him, he had most of the empty boxes gathered in his strong arms. "If you're referring to your ancestor, I have no doubt he availed himself of a bath at the horse trough."

Her mouth curved upward. "But the water wouldn't have been heated."

"If the day was as hot for him as ours has been, he probably wished the lukewarm water had been a lot colder." On that note he disappeared from the kitchen.

She found herself wondering if Nikos would take a hot or cold shower. But that kind of thinking was making chaos of her emotions.

Time to take advantage of his brief absence and head for the bathroom. She grabbed the towels and bath mat. Everything else she needed was in her cosmetics bag.

Not until she stepped in the tub did she realize there was no shower curtain. The only thing to do was place the mat right up against the outside of the tub. When she washed her hair, she would have to be careful not to get too much of the spray on the floor.

She'd brought mango body wash with her. It was her favorite scent. Once she'd finished her shower and brushed her teeth, she opened the little window to let out some of the steam. At this point the bathroom felt more like a sauna.

One thing she could say for shorter hair. It would dry a lot faster. She brushed it into some semblance of her feather cut, then slipped on a sleeveless, knee-length cotton nightie in pale pink with scalloped edges.

For decency's sake she put on a short-sleeved cotton blouse which would have to serve as a robe of sorts. Her actual robe was too transparent. Before leaving Buffalo, she hadn't known she'd end up sleeping in the same room with Nikos.

She repacked her clothes and shoes so nothing was left in the bathroom. Nikos would need all the space available for his things.

Upon reaching the deserted living room, she discovered he'd put the fan in there. Still refreshed from her shower, she put her suitcase down and stood in front of it for a moment, letting the breeze cool her limbs.

Nikos stood against the closed door where he'd just come from locking up the truck's cab. He couldn't move.

For one thing Tracey's fragrance had assailed him. For another, the sight of her in bare feet with her modest nightgown billowing around those shapely legs did more to raise his blood pressure than anything else could have done.

There was an allure about a young woman who wasn't aware of her beauty. Coupled with her vulnerability, which she fought so hard to keep hidden, he felt himself caught in an invisible net, drawing him in, slowly, inexorably. For the first time in his life, he didn't feel like fighting its pull. On the contrary…

But he had to remember she was holding out

for a proposal of marriage. All this pretense of entering into a business arrangement was an act!

He would use a contact to phone Schiller's and find out if she'd really been a student there. Probably a Celine Calvet had attended and Tracey had picked the name to make her story ring true. But a picture ID sent to his e-mail would solve the mystery, wig or no wig.

Nikos didn't doubt her marriage had proved to be a mistake. It must have fallen apart as soon as she'd realized her prince couldn't aggrandize her wealth. Like Paul, she was driven by greed. But being a female, her methods were different. Find a man with more money than her grandfather.

She was determined to become Nikos's wife. Knowing how to bewitch a man, she'd clung to him a little while ago, allowing him to feel every curve of her luscious body.

With hardened resolve not to let her get past his defenses again, he locked the front door. "While I shower, I'll leave you to decide which bed you want."

He heard a soft gasp before she spun around, giving him a frontal view of flushed cheeks and the blouse that couldn't hide the mold of the tempting figure beneath. Her normally wide mouth, still red though it was minus any lipstick, had formed an O of surprise.

"I—I'll take the one nearest the door."

If he read that stammer correctly, she hadn't known he'd been standing there watching her.

Her eyes glowed like two green turquoises, an impossible color only nature could achieve. The little pulse at her throat throbbed in sync with his pulse.

Over the years, her image had played in the recesses of his mind like a tantalizing apparition cavorting in and out of the far distant swells. A shape of crimson and quicksilver that beckoned, then eluded, preventing him from coming near enough to catch hold. Until now…

"We're going to have to be up early."

She nodded. "Farmer's hours."

Farmer's hours. That meant more time to be awake with her, working at her side. Then early to bed…

A negative burst of adrenaline caused him to reach for his suitcase and head for the bathroom. By the time he was ready for bed, he'd stayed in there longer than planned.

With the bathroom redolent of her cosmetics, he couldn't help but entertain certain intimate thoughts of the two of them. As a result, he'd stood beneath the hot water until long after it had run out. It was just as well he'd finished up taking a cold shower.

By the time he'd shaved and donned shorts and a T-shirt, he felt prepared to a degree to be in the same room with her and stay in some sort of control. He'd thought he was a man who could temper his passion. But that was before Tracey had trumped his ace by pretending that this whole business setup had been exactly what she'd wanted.

She was good.

When he left the bathroom, he turned out lights but noticed she'd left the one on in the living room. He wasn't pleased to see she was still awake.

She lay on her side so he could make out the undulating lines of her body outlined beneath the sheet. Those fabulous blue-green eyes were watching him beneath a swirl of glistening red hair. During her seven-year marriage to Karl Von Axel, he'd had the legal right to do whatever he'd wanted with her.

Nikos drew in a torturous breath and went in the kitchen for two bottles of water. When he came back, he put one on the floor next to her before turning out the light.

"Thank you, Nikos. I was just thinking about getting up to do that."

In front of him, of course, in order to tantalize him. "Then I've saved you a trip."

Remembering her near mishap, which even he doubted she could have staged, Nikos sat down on the cot with care. Hoping to have made the circumstances so uninviting she'd give up, he couldn't complain about the situation he'd created. Leaving the blanket at the foot, he drew the sheet over his legs and lay back.

"This is fun," she said unexpectedly.

"I assure you the novelty will wear off."

By tomorrow night she'd be long gone from Greece, having failed to attain her goal. But he had to admit he was surprised she'd lasted this long.

"I've been worrying about that. You've put your whole life on hold to help me."

An actress worthy of the Dionysus Theater in Athens.

"This is my home. The fact that you happen to be here with me is only coincidental."

"You know what I meant. I realize this is your birthplace, but you live in Athens."

"Not any longer."

"You mean until the six months are up?"

"I mean for good."

He heard her sheet rustle. "What are you saying?" The slight tremor in her voice pleased him no end.

"I've decided to retire."

"*Retire*—" Her shock told him all he needed to know. "At thirty-eight?"

"Age is relative."

"It's still so young, Nikos!"

She sounded frantic at the thought of him not bringing in any more money.

"I always planned to come back one day, and have been actively making preparations to carry out this move for the last twelve months."

"But *here?*"

"Where else? Life has become a treadmill for me. It's not the way I want to live it. After a lot of thought I decided to get off. You have no

idea how I've yearned for the peace and tranquility of the farm."

"You don't like business?"

"It was a means to an end. If circumstances
had been different, I would never have left it in
the first place. But I didn't have a choice at the
time.

"When my business took off, I didn't think
about going at such a hectic pace. I was a driven
man, but no longer. The good news is, I've taken
the steps to close my company doors and give all
my worldly goods to medical research."

She was quiet for so long he wondered if he
hadn't given her a heart attack. He smirked to
think her scheme to entrap him was fast turning
into a nightmare.

"I want to see my money spent coming up with
new low-cost medicines to fight infections peni-
cillin won't touch."

"Did your mother die of an infection?"

"Yes."

"I'm so sorry," came her tremulous voice.

"It would have been preventable if my father
hadn't been too poor to buy the needed drugs."

Finally she said, "I can understand your desire

to help people, but what's happened to make you take this drastic step now, Nikos?"

"Last year I was in Tasmania when I had another birthday and decided time was fleeting. I woke up that morning and thought, what am I doing here? I'd much rather be at home."

"What will you do?" She sounded as if it were the end of her world.

"Get married and raise four or five little farmers."

"Be serious." Her voice shook.

"You think I'm not? I always wanted a big family. They'll work the farm and learn the meaning of hard work the way I did. After I'm dead they can divide it up if they want, but I don't plan to leave them anything else. It would be their ruination."

"Isn't that a little harsh?" she asked quietly.

It was a good thing he couldn't see the agony on her face or he might have burst out laughing.

"Let's consider what all your grandfather's money did for you," he drove the point home with relish.

"At twenty-five you've never earned your own living. You're already divorced from a prince. There's a long trail of sponging ex-lovers behind you, no children to comfort you in your old age. Sadly you're more needy than ever now that Loretto's stock isn't as valuable as before.

"Women may envy you, and men desire you, yet we both know you're only a lost little rich girl. Albeit one who's a tad less rich now, and could end up in the poorhouse if Loretto's continues to go downhill.

"I have no intention of letting any of that happen to my children, male or female. As the good book says, they'll earn their daily bread and work for every dime by the sweat of their brow all the days of their life."

More silence ensued.

"Does this mean you have your future wife picked out?"

He groaned to realize the sweet, innocent Tracey he'd once known had grown into a fully fledged narcissist.

"You mean a woman who will work side by side with me, bear our children, be content with our lot and love only me whatever life brings?"

"Yes."

"Once long ago there was such a person."

"What happened?" she cried softly.

"Circumstances prevented us from getting together."

"Was she beautiful?"

"She had an inner beauty, an almost spiritual essence that appealed to me."

"Then she wasn't one of the women to share your bed?"

"She wasn't that kind of woman."

"Have you always loved her?" she whispered the question.

"Let's just say she owns a piece of my heart, but that doesn't mean I haven't met several other women who please me. As soon as I've built a house on my favorite spot of ground, I'll get married."

"W-Where is that special spot?" her voice faltered.

"I thought you understood. The farm of course."

"But what of this farmhouse?" Again he heard alarm in her voice.

"Don't worry. You'll be back in New York by the time I've incorporated it into the new one. When everything's built, I'll have stone floors put in these common rooms. The roof will be replaced with lattice work, turning the old family home into a patio.

"It will serve as an extension of the main house where my family can enjoy being outside in the cooler months."

He heard her breath catch. "That's a really wonderful idea, Nikos. To incorporate your family home into the new one sounds lovely. You'll have tangible proof of your roots to show your children."

Her response wasn't the one he'd expected. But then she was still playing him along, not believing a word he said because she was convinced she would soon be wearing his wedding ring on her finger.

"Y-You've waited a long time to get married." The crack in Tracey's voice was the most satisfying sound he'd heard all night.

"That's right."

"Because of her."

"Yes, plus the fact that I had to find myself first. Until now I haven't had anything of value to offer a woman."

"How can you say that?" she cried.

"I'm not talking about money. Unfortunately

you wouldn't understand." In truth he envied what his brother had. A loving wife, children, a home.

The quiet resounded in his ears.

"Are you going to choose a woman from Kalambaka?"

He had her squirming now. Hopefully she'd end this charade about wanting to be a business-woman and leave Greece to go husband hunting elsewhere.

"Go to sleep, Tracey. Morning will be here before you know it, and I'm exhausted."

Go to sleep?

After you've told me you're planning to be married soon?

Tracey couldn't bear it. Her pain went too deep for tears. She moved to a fetal position, crushing the pillow to her chest to withstand the tremors of her body. The next thing she knew, voices outside the farmhouse reached her ears.

Nikos's brother? Any other sounds she heard came from her stomach, reminding her she hadn't eaten a proper meal since lunch yesterday.

She turned on her other side and opened her eyes. Nikos was already up, but his cot was still unmade.

Sunlight streamed in the front window. Despite the fan that was still operating, the house was hot.

One glance at her watch proclaimed it was 9:00 a.m. Greek time. Her first day on the job as a farmer and already she wasn't doing her part. After what Nikos had told her last night, she'd wanted to die and hadn't been able to fall asleep for hours.

She was getting used to the hurtful things he had to say to her. But the revelation that he was planning to settle down soon had the effect of carving her heart into pieces.

Tears rolled down her face. When she'd first met Nikos, she'd wanted to belong to him. She'd wanted to grow up and have his babies, make a home for him and their children. The life he'd sketched out had spoken to her soul.

But it was never meant to be. He'd always loved someone else. The only reason he'd brought Tracey here was that his innate goodness had prevailed, allowing her to do something worthy with her pitiful life. It was all up to her.

Even if she couldn't have his love, if she could prove herself in his eyes, then maybe she could win his respect. It wouldn't be everything she wanted from him, but she couldn't imagine going through life knowing he despised her. That would be too great a burden to carry.

Before he came back inside, she needed to get ready and never let him know how much she was suffering. One day years from now she hoped to meet him again when she was the chairman of the board at Loretto's. Then maybe she would see something in his eyes besides disdain.

Sliding carefully off the bed, she reached for her suitcase and darted through the house to the bathroom. After showering last night, she didn't have to do much to make herself presentable.

She dressed in the same white pants she'd worn last evening, but put on a sage-green top with cap sleeves, cool and lightweight. Once her sandals were on and her hair brushed, she hurried to the back porch where she could hear more voices, thinking she'd find Nikos.

When she opened the door, she discovered two men installing a new washer and dryer. While they kept working, they smiled and said a greeting in Greek.

She thanked them, all the while blessing Nikos under her breath. When he'd said they were going to be farmers, she hadn't known how far he planned to imitate her ancestor's humble beginnings.

After shutting the door, she hurried down the hall. As she reached the dining room she saw some more deliverymen at the front door bringing in a refrigerator on a dolly. Behind them came a stove on another dolly pushed by a third man.

Nikos, dressed in cream-colored jeans and a white T-shirt, brought up the rear carrying an air conditioner in his arms. He set it down near the window. No matter how distant he was to her, she was glad to see he didn't want them dying of the heat.

"There's one for each room. By the time we get home from town, the house should be cool enough to be comfortable."

"How soon are we leaving?" she asked without looking at him.

He probably had several girlfriends in town. Now that he'd moved to the farm, he'd be able to see them all the time. The picture of him with any desirable woman had the power to crucify Tracey.

"First rule of a farmer. Eat a hearty breakfast. Over a meal in town we'll make out a list of supplies to buy."

While he brought in the other air conditioners, she made up their beds and stowed their suitcases at each end. Reaching for her purse, she walked outside past the delivery vans to the pickup truck and waited for him.

An unrelenting sun beat down on her from a clear blue sky. How many thousands of mornings had Nikos and his brother followed their father out the door to face this exact scene in preparation for a hard day's work in the fields?

Shielding her eyes with her hand, she tried to imagine the barren ground under cultivation from her own efforts. The image refused to come.

Nikos joined her and unlocked the door of the cab. "It looks daunting now, but with a lot of hard work, you ought to be able to make this place flourish."

After he helped her inside the truck, she said, "I've been thinking about this heat. Please don't laugh at me, but wouldn't it be better to farm in the middle of the night?"

"Cooler maybe," he answered, "but under cover of darkness there's always the danger of sowing wild oats instead of mustard seed."

In spite of his mocking rejoinder, her body

quickened because she'd been in danger of wanting to do the former with him for years now. But last night any faint hope of that ever happening had died.

"Maybe I'll end up adding wild oats to Loretto's product line."

"It'll be your crop to do with as you please."

He didn't believe she could do it, but she'd made up her mind to prove him wrong, even if it killed her.

"How long do you think it will take to grow one?"

"Eighty to eighty-five days." Only that long? "By then you should have learned enough to make informed comments at the board meetings."

But that meant she'd only be with him three months, not six!

He was cutting the time frame in half they would be working together so he could put his personal plans into motion. Stabbing pain almost paralyzed her.

She moistened her lips that had gone dry suddenly. "Isn't this your brother's property, too?"

"Was. I bought his half from him."

"After you decided to come home."

He nodded.

"D-Does he know about me?"

"Why should he? We don't keep track of each other's day-to-day business."

"He'll think the worst when he learns I'm living here."

"Whatever opinion he has of you would have already been formed after following your exploits in the press over the last few years."

Don't ask any more personal questions, Tracey. His answers are tearing you up inside.

"How big is the farm altogether?"

"Three acres including the land the farmhouse stands on. You'll be working one acre."

Only three to feed and clothe a family of four year in and year out? She lowered her head. "Your father had to make every minute of the day count, didn't he?"

"That's right. Sometimes the elements worked against him and there was little harvest for his efforts. In the end, all his hard work still wasn't enough."

For the drugs his mother had needed.

A shadow had crossed over his face. Nikos had

to be remembering those black times. A parent's illness was traumatic.

"How did your brother feel about selling?"

"He was happy with the price before he found out I was the buyer. Does that answer your question?"

"It's often that way in families. They pretend not to care who gets what until they're put to the test. Human nature I guess."

He darted her a speaking glance. "You certainly didn't have that problem. All those millions came to you with no siblings resenting you for your fair share. Fortunately for you, you don't have a family to feed on your one acre in case it's a bad year for mustard crops."

Tracey could have bitten her tongue out for saying anything. "If I brought up a sensitive subject, forgive me. I was thinking how nice it would have been if I'd had a big brother growing up." Someone to protect her from her grandfather. Someone to help her and her mother escape from his terrible reach.

The truck unexpectedly accelerated. "There's nothing to forgive, but let's agree to leave the discussion of brothers alone, yours or mine."

CHAPTER FIVE

ANY HOPE THAT NIKOS WOULD BE in a better mood this morning because he was leaving business behind in preparation for a future personal life, was nonexistent. It was Tracey's taciturn mentor who drove the rest of the short trip with an inscrutable expression on his hard-boned features.

On the outskirts of town she spied a fascinating-looking graveyard with all-white stones and crosses, a place she'd love to wander through when she had the time.

They passed several road shrines and a statue of the king of Sparta with patches of lavender flowers sprouting up between them in no particular order. She watched dark-haired children skipping along the road eating ice-cream cones in their shorts and tank tops.

Yesterday she'd seen Kalambaka from the air.

This morning she had a different vantage point from the valley floor. It sat on the edge of the plain below the Meteora that formed the backdrop and looked enormous.

The town's charming main street was lined with small hotels, sidewalk cafés and little shops bearing striped awnings. Tracey caught sight of several that displayed Greek icons and rows of worry beads in a riot of colors.

Nikos slowed down and wedged them into a spot between two parked cars. She waited for a scraping sound, but it didn't come. "I don't know how you did that."

"You would have to be born here." The tone in his voice indicated his dark mood was still with him.

Two steps from their truck was one of those picturesque outdoor tavernas. She jumped out of the cab before Nikos could help her.

The less physical touching that went on between them, the better for her peace of mind. Despite his coldness, every time his arm or hip happened to brush against hers, she grew more aware of him and couldn't throw off the effect of one more layer of contact.

He put his hand behind her waist to usher her past the tables packed with tourists, sending a lick of flame through her body. "Inviting as this looks, I prefer to eat inside where it's cooler."

"So do I." Between Nikos and the heat, she was on the verge of catching fire.

The second they entered the café, the man at the counter broke out in a wide grin and raced around to hug Nikos. Obviously they were old friends. After introducing Tracey, Nikos and the older man broke into a spate of rapid Greek.

He nodded and showed them to a spot behind some long beads at the rear of the room. It turned out to be a private eating area, almost cold compared to the rest of the café. She had a feeling it was where the staff ate.

"I'll make certain no one bothers you." He winked at Tracey before leaving them alone.

Her delicately shaped eyebrows lifted. "Old-time farming perks?"

"That's right," he answered in a civil tone, not willing to enter into any levity. "I told him we haven't had a solid meal since yesterday afternoon."

For the next fifteen minutes they were treated

to a series of breakfast dishes that probably put five pounds on her.

"Enough," she cried when Nikos offered her the last cherry from the fresh fruit plate.

"Can't have you fainting the first day on the job."

"I'm not the type. Nikos? Before we go, there's something I've been wanting to ask you. Could we talk for a little while?"

"As long as it doesn't take too long. We've got other things to do while we're in town."

She knew that. He was probably counting the minutes until he could get her started on a project that would leave him some freedom to do what he really wanted.

"You've told me about Emilio Loretto, but I'd like to hear about the beginnings of Nikos Lazaridis. What happened to you after you left the farm years ago? What *was* the idea you came up with that made your fortune?"

His eyes narrowed on her mouth where she could still taste the cherry juice. "My fortune... You really don't know?"

She would always be suspect in his eyes.

"I realize it had to do with farming, but when I showed an interest in you, Grandfather changed the subject. End of discussion. With hindsight I can see his jealousy of you ate him alive. The more I tried to find out about you, the more he was determined to say nothing."

Nikos grimaced. Maybe she was getting through to him. Or maybe he thought she was feeding him lies to win his sympathy.

"One time when I found out you'd come to the mansion, I planned a little picnic for you. I asked one of the maids to slip you a message that said to meet me behind the topiary maze below the west terrace."

His eyes flickered. "I never got it."

"That doesn't surprise me. I had it all ready for you in my secret place with foods I was sure you would love. But one of the gardeners saw what I was doing and went straight to my grandfather. Instead of it being you who found me waiting, Grandfather showed up.

"Without saying a word, he marched me to my bedroom and locked me in."

"He really did that?"

Oh why was she bothering—

"Yes. He told me he'd let me out when I learned to know my place. After he unlocked the door the next day, I learned the maid had been fired. My mother begged me not to seek you out again for fear everyone would feel his wrath.

"From then on I only talked to you when Grandfather permitted it and could be there with us. He decided what we would talk about."

Nikos had to know she was telling the truth because he'd been there. His jaw grew taut. "I'm sorry if you got into trouble because of me."

"I got into trouble for simply being alive, Nikos. It's been following me ever since. I've only told you this to explain why I'm asking questions about you now."

Her explanation seemed to give Nikos pause before he said, "I went to Athens and did any job I could to put me through college."

"So you got a degree."

"Yes."

"Grandfather never finished college. That explains why he was always trying to compete with you. What did you major in?"

"Engineering. While there I developed a machine to crush seeds."

"Why was that so important?"

He studied her for a moment. "When you

reduce a seed to powder, or flour as some call it, then you've created the potential for several new products the seed farmer can sell.

"I showed my invention to some people who invested in my idea, and I started up my first manufacturing business.

"At first I sold them within the country, then traveled to other countries, talking to farmers, demonstrating my product. Did you know for example that more than seven hundred million pounds of mustard are consumed worldwide each year?"

Tracey shook her head. "I had no idea. I don't even like mustard that much."

"Those who do have kept you in a lifestyle few people will ever enjoy," he drawled.

"I'm aware of that. Please. Just for once would you treat me like I don't completely disgust you. I truly do want to know."

After drinking the rest of his coffee, he said, "Consider that mustard is only one type of seed. There are many others with a variety of uses. I was lucky to happen on to the scene when I did. A market was waiting, and the business took off."

Tracey's admiration for Nikos knew no limits. "An overnight success."

"Hardly. When I came to the States, I met your grandfather. He was already using a crushing machine invented in your country. But after trying mine, he was converted because it did something the other one didn't."

"What was that?" Tracey couldn't hear enough.

"Mustard, especially the Oriental and brown types, should be grown on land with as little wild mustard as possible to avoid costs of removal and loss of tame mustard seeds. But when wild mustard seed does exist, my machine can mechanically separate it from the larger-seeded yellow type."

He unexpectedly pushed his chair away from the table. "After we buy groceries and some work clothes, we'll stop by the grain and seed co-op. If you're willing to learn, that's where your real education is going to begin."

He still wasn't convinced.

She watched him put some bills on the table, then he stood up to assist her. They left the taverna and walked out to the truck.

Three hours later they were on their way back

to the farm. Tracey's head was spinning from all the information she'd tried to assimilate. After Nikos had introduced her to the manager of the co-op, who spoke passable English, he'd left them alone with no explanation of where he was going. But she knew.

"Tell me what you've gleaned so far," he asked as they drove away. Her final purchase of the day had been put in the back of the truck along with their other shopping bags.

Nikos was in a much better mood than before, otherwise he wouldn't be asking her questions. She should be happy about it, but inside she was writhing in torment to think he might have been with some woman who was important to him.

"Well, I discovered that yellow mustard is usually used for prepared or table mustard, or as a condiment. Then there's dry mustard, frequently used as a seasoning in mayonnaise, salad dressings and sauces."

"What else?"

"Let's see… Flour made from yellow mustard is an excellent emulsifying agent and stabilizer, used in sausage preparation. Brown and Oriental mustards are also used as oilseed crops."

"How many kinds of mustard seeds did he show you?"

"Eight. I had no idea there were that many."

"There are infinite varieties sold all over the world."

"So I understand." There'd been too much to take in. Her brain was exploding.

On their way out of town, she turned to him. "Did your father grow any other crops besides mustard?"

"Cotton and potatoes."

Such a clipped response. Anything to do with his family made him defensive. Tracey's curiosity about his past life was going to get her into trouble, so she lapsed into silence.

When they arrived back at the farmhouse, she saw a different van parked along the track. The Greek writing on the side didn't tell her anything.

She turned to Nikos. "Were you expecting another delivery?"

"That would be my brother's van from the hotel." He didn't sound pleased.

They pulled in front of the van and got out. Tracey climbed down from the cab in time to see a tall, attractive young man with dark hair who could be seventeen or eighteen, coming around the side of the farmhouse wearing dark pants and a white shirt.

He bore a slight resemblance to Nikos. Since he couldn't be his brother, he had to be a nephew.

The two of them hugged. Then the young man's eyes fastened on Tracey. To her dismay, they lit up. He must have recognized her from the tabloids because he muttered something to Nikos in Greek with an excitement she understood all too well.

"Speak English, Ari. May I introduce Ms. Loretto. This is my nephew, Ari."

"How do you do, Ari." She shook his hand. "It's very nice to meet you. Actually my last name is Conner now. After my divorce I took back my father's name. Since you and Nikos are related, I'd rather you called me Tracey."

If Nikos didn't like it, that was too bad.

Ari smiled. "No problem, Tracey. I saw you and Uncle Nikos on television last night. You're even more beautiful in person."

There was no escaping the evil eye of the press. The two of them had been seen leaving the yacht, and eating at the restaurant in the Plaka.

"Thank you."

His fascinated gaze darted back and forth between her and Nikos, who stood along the sidelines like a spectator.

"Papa said you've come home for good. Are you and Tracey getting married?"

"No—" she blurted so fast she saw astonishment written on both their faces. Whatever Nikos had told or not told his family about his future plans, she didn't dare speak out of turn. But she had to say something that would explain her presence and not make Nikos look bad.

"I asked your uncle for a huge business favor. He has kindly agreed to be my mentor and teach me to farm."

That got Arui's attention in a hurry.

"You?"

She laughed gently. *"Me."*

Moving closer to Ari she said, "I don't blame you for being incredulous, but it's something I need to learn. He's giving me three months of his valuable time, then I'll be returning to New York to take my place at Loretto's."

Ari was clearly puzzled. His hands went to his hips. "Why would you want to work when you don't have to?"

"I can't imagine a more boring existence."

He shook his head and grinned. "If I had millions of American dollars to spend for the rest of my life…"

"It would be a meaningless waste," she assured him.

"You sound like Uncle Nikos."

"Then trust both of us because we know what we're talking about."

His eyes narrowed on her features the way Nikos's eyes sometimes did, except Ari's twinkled. "I'm going to have to come over and watch this miracle happen."

"With your brilliant uncle guiding me, I won't need one, but I'd love some help if you're offering."

"Me?" His arms spread apart in a helpless gesture.

"Have *you* ever farmed?"

"No. I plan to go into the hotel business."

"Good for you. But just remember the blood of a farming family runs through your veins. Why not drop by when you can and learn with me? We'll have fun. Who knows? You might discover you actually like it."

His eyes danced. "I think the rumors about you are true. You are a little crazy, Tracey."

She didn't take offense because unlike his uncle, Ari meant none. "Take it from me, I'm a lot crazy."

They both laughed.

Crazy like a fox.

Tracey might have won this battle, but she would lose the war, Nikos vowed through gritted teeth. Before another day had gone by, she would have taken off in pursuit of easier prey.

He undid the back of the truck to unload the secondhand dresser he'd purchased. In fairness to Tracey, she hadn't made any complaints, but he didn't like living out of a suitcase any longer.

"Let me help," Ari said as an afterthought. He was so mesmerized by Tracey, he looked dazed and had forgotten Nikos was even there.

His nephew was at an age where the attention of one of the world's most infamous, wealthy females had already flattered him to the point he imagined himself in love.

Hell. This was one scenario he hadn't counted on when he'd come up with his plan.

After they walked into the living room and set the dresser down next to Nikos's bed, Ari whistled. "This place looks like an old World War II outpost."

"Except that this barracks has air-conditioning. I love it," Tracy said, bringing a box of groceries into the kitchen.

Nikos brought in more boxes, amazed to hear the two of them chattering like a pair of magpies who'd been sitting in the same tree for years.

She sounded so delighted with everything, she had Ari convinced. Bowled over, to be precise.

Nikos's nephew didn't know which side was up. It was time to remind him.

"Ari? If you want to make yourself useful, come out on the back porch and help me with the washing machine."

"I'll be right there, Uncle."

Right there turned into five minutes. "Sorry. I was helping Tracey put all the food away. She's invited me for dinner."

"Did you tell her you had to get back to the hotel?"

"I phoned Papa on my cell. He said I could stay. He'll be by to see you soon. Mama wants you and

Tracey to have dinner at the hotel with us next week after you're settled in. You pick the night."

Much as Nikos had wanted his space, maybe it was better to get all this out of the way now. "I'll let your mother know."

He looked up from the side of the washing machine where he'd been trying to find the most level spot of flooring. "Did Tracey tell you what she's fixing?"

"No. She asked me to translate some of the labels."

"You'd be better off telling her you have to get back to work on an emergency."

"I don't care if she can't cook."

No. You wouldn't…

"She's only twenty-five, right?"

"And you're only seventeen."

"I'll be eighteen next month."

"Forget what you're thinking, Ari."

He winked at Nikos. "The way she looks, that wouldn't be possible. How come there's no one like her around here?"

"Come on. You know the answer to that."

"I'm not talking about her money. She's nice, Uncle Nikos. Funny, too. I can't figure out why she's divorced. That prince must have been nuts to let her go."

"She let *him* go." Tracey didn't know how to remain faithful to one man.

"Actually she said he wanted it."

Nikos frowned. "She told you that?"

"I asked her if she was still missing him. She said they'd been friends in the marriage, but he thought they'd be better friends divorced. Even if it was a lie, which I don't think it was, she didn't make him out to be a monster. Most celebrities bash their exes.

"Like I said, she's totally different from the way she's portrayed in the news. When I asked her how she felt about you, she told me a secret."

A deeper scowl marred Nikos's features. "Then you should keep it."

"She said she's much more terrified of failing in front of you than in front of her board back in New York, so cut her some slack, Uncle Nikos. I don't know anybody who *likes* to farm except you.

"Now I'd better go in and help her. She admitted she's never cooked Greek food and said she might need my assistance. I take it she doesn't want you going to bed grouchy because you're hungry."

The woman was a master of manipulation. Ari had become putty in her hands.

Five hours later, Nikos walked back in the house after seeing Ari off and discovered Tracey at the dining-room table. The dishes were done and now she was working in her new ledger, surrounded by some farming books he'd bought her printed in English.

Curious to know what she'd recorded, he walked behind her and looked over her shoulder. It was a mistake. The feminine scent of the shampoo clinging to her hair caused him to breathe in sharply.

He looked down the list of the things they'd bought that she'd entered. "I'm glad to see you've taken my advice and recorded everything. Your taxes will be based on this record. A farmer is as much an accountant as a worker of the soil, entering every debit or credit. But since we wear T-shirts and jeans anyway, you can't include them as part of your farming expenses."

"Oh. I didn't know that." She quickly erased the entry.

His eyes traveled farther down. "I see four thousand dollars for seeds in the debit column."

"Yes. I was told anywhere from three to fourteen pounds could be used to plant an acre, so I bought fourteen just to be safe. You know, in case some spilled and there was an accident or something. That means 286 dollars a pound, which seemed like a real bargain."

"Tracey—" Before he could stop himself, his hands had fallen on her shoulders. He felt the warmth of her flesh through the cotton material of her T-shirt. "I don't know where you got that figure."

Her body started to tremble. "It's on the sales slip right here."

Forcing himself to let go of her before he acted on feelings that were exploding out of control, he took the paper from her hand to see for himself. When he realized what she'd done, his eyes closed tightly.

"That's the number of the bin."

"Oh."

"The seeds cost three dollars and eighty cents a pound, but the receipt is made out in Euros. He billed us for fifty-three dollars and twenty cents."

She jerked around in the chair and looked up

at him in astonishment. "That's all it costs for the seed?"

Tracey didn't have a clue. "Yes. If you'd actually spent four thousand American dollars, there would be at least a hundred pounds of seed in the back of the truck, enough to plant ten acres."

Her features crumpled. "I'm a fool aren't I? Go ahead and laugh. I know you want to, and I wouldn't blame you if you did. But I'm going to learn this if it kills me."

In the next instant, she turned back around and erased the figure to put in the one he'd just dictated. With her shoulders hunched, and her body held rigid, she reminded him of the young woman who'd stood there and taken a verbal chastising from her grandfather in front of Nikos.

The painful memory sucked all the amusement from him. When his father had first taken him and Leon into town, Nikos hadn't known the price of seed either.

He couldn't believe she was continuing to pursue this.

"What kind of seeds did you end up buying?"

"After the manager explained the types he

carried, he left it up to me to decide which variety to choose. After considering everything, and agonizing over my choice, I decided to buy Gilsilba."

"Why?"

"Because it's a yellow mustard whose crop matures faster. I figured you want to be rid of me within three months so that made sense. I also learned that yellow mustard doesn't shatter as easily during the harvesting, so I'm presuming there will be less crop to lose. If it ever comes up," she added in a dull voice.

"Time will tell," he baited her.

She averted her eyes. "He said anything from three to fourteen pounds an acre would work. At one hundred thousand seeds a pound for that particular variety, I figured I would need a lot because the crop might not be substantial."

"Why do you say that?"

"Because he said it should have been planted in the spring, and I'm getting a late start. I thought it better to buy more than less."

For someone who knew absolutely nothing about farming, she was showing a natural instinct that surprised him.

"When Elias comes to help you till the soil

and pack it, don't forget to figure in the cost of his hours."

"Why pack it? How come the ground can't just be tilled and then planted? It would save money."

"Because a firmly packed seedbed with adequate moisture allows shallow planting, which is what you want. A half-inch depth encourages rapid, uniform seed germination and emergence of seedlings. Cutting corners results in a less fruitful crop. A few of those, and a farmer could go under."

Her eyes suddenly searched his with what appeared to be grave concern. "Did your father ever have to cut some of the steps because he couldn't afford it?"

The question seemed to come out of nowhere and hit him squarely in the gut. "Most of the time."

"Oh Nikos—" Her eyes glistened with tears. "Your poor father."

She closed the ledger and got up from the table. "This is a whole new world to me. In one day I've learned more about one tiny aspect of farming than I've learned in twenty-five years of living. Excuse me while I take my shower."

Ready to erupt with a jumble of feelings he didn't dare examine right now, Nikos moved in the opposite direction and found himself outside. Without conscious thought, he walked over to the truck and climbed in the bed to examine the seed she'd bought.

In truth, he'd expected her to bolt after breakfast. He'd purposely left the truck with her in case she'd decided to take off, leaving him a note of goodbye at the co-op.

His shock at discovering she'd spent several hours there talking with the manager was almost as great as the reality of this purchase. His fingers sifted through the seeds she'd thought had cost several thousand dollars.

As Ari had said, she was funny.

Funny-dangerous. The greatest quick study he'd ever known. It shouldn't have surprised him. He ground his teeth. She had the Loretto genes.

Just wait until tomorrow when the manual labor began. He'd break her yet.

When he returned to the farmhouse, she was already in bed. She'd put water bottles by both their cots.

"Your nephew is wonderful, Nikos. So natural and charming. And a good cook, too. He's offered to give me lessons."

"Anything except to help on the farm."

"I've got *you* for that."

His heart rate accelerated without his permission. "I have to shower."

A few minutes later he felt a little fresher. After turning off all the lights, he lay down on his bed without the benefit of the sheet.

"Nikos?"

"Elias will be here early in the morning to start work, Tracey. Better get to sleep if you don't want to be dragging tomorrow."

"I will, but you have no idea how excited I am. When I left New York, I didn't know what was going to happen. You could have been in Africa or South America. And even if I was lucky enough to catch up with you in Europe, I wasn't at all sure you would agree to help me.

"You don't just intrude on Nikos Lazaridis, of all people. You don't expect to get close to him. That's why I gave the waiter such a big tip."

"Somehow you managed." He covered his eyes with his arm. "I came to you the week before, remember?"

"That was a duty visit because of Mother, and you always do your duty because you're an honorable man. It's a rare quality my father possessed, too."

"You're wrong about me, Tracey."

"No I'm not. I haven't forgotten the tongue lashing my grandfather gave me in front of you years ago because of my dog. It was humiliating and painful for me to be reprimanded while a stranger was looking on."

The incident had never left Nikos's mind. This lovely girl-woman with flaming red hair and a porcelain-like complexion had suddenly appeared in the drive. Until she'd hurried toward him, he'd thought he'd seen a vision. Then she was standing in front of him and he could see the hurt in her beautiful eyes, making everything too real….

She'd looked so shattered and frightened at her grandfather's dressing down. Yet when she'd fastened her gaze on Nikos, who'd been holding Samson, it had seemed as if their souls had exchanged a conversation that transcended words.

Inexplicably, love for her had been born that day. He'd wanted to spirit her away in his arms and take care of her forever.

Nikos had never assaulted anyone, but at that

moment he'd come close to putting his hands around the old man's neck.

When Tracey had told him about the picnic she'd once planned for them, he'd felt as if he'd been kicked in the gut and thrown into the River Styx. Something warned him she hadn't been lying about her grandfather. It had made him realize she'd been subjected to that mean-spiritedness her whole life.

"Admit you haven't forgotten what he did, Nikos."

"Neither have you, obviously."

"Don't worry. I had my mother. Together we made it through the dark times."

How many were there, Tracey?

"You were so nice to her. She would have been thrilled to know you brought those beautiful flowers to our door the other day.

"I want you to know something, Nikos. When you held my dog and played with him despite my grandfather's dislike of the situation, you won a friend for life."

"You mean Samson."

"Him, too, but I meant *me*. I vowed that one day I would find a way to repay you." She gave a self-deprecating laugh. "Now look what I've done. You've had to rescue me again. At this rate I'm going to be indebted to you forever."

His guts ached for the hard life she'd had to live at the hands of Paul Loretto. But that girl was gone and she'd turned into a woman whose lifestyle had sickened him to the depths of his soul. So how to explain her behavior with him now? He'd sell his soul to know what part was real.

"All these years I've planned to get back at my grandfather by proving a female member of the family could be every bit as valuable as he was in business.

"Mother cheered me on. She was my great comfort and promised to be there for me. But life played its tricks on me. You know what that feels like. You lost your mother, too."

Remembered pain made him realize the raw pain in her voice couldn't have been manufactured.

"Since then I've learned that if you're going to reach for a dream, you have to do it on your own. The way *you* did, Nikos. I'm in awe of you for that. As for myself, I admit I'm frightened of failure."

Her words reminded him of his earlier conversation with Ari.

"I've talked big all these years. Today I had to step up to the plate and put my money where my mouth is. You know…choosing which seeds to buy.

"All those clichés about finding out what I'm *really* made of have hit home. For the first time in my life I'm standing outside myself, and I can't see my reflection clearly. I thought I knew myself so well, but it's like looking at a stranger.

"But you wouldn't know what I'm talking about. When you left Kalambaka years ago, you knew exactly who you were, what you were doing. You had vision."

Like hell.

"That was because you're Helios."

Nikos groaned inwardly. "He never existed."

"I didn't believe it either."

"And now you do."

"Yes. You have the uncanny power to understand what makes another person tick. You know things instinctively."

I wish I did, my little mermaid.

"Have you ever been unsure of yourself?"

If he had, it was because of the complex woman lying a few yards away from him. "Let's just say that with the passing years, I'm more at home in my own skin. Your fun is just beginning. You said it yourself to Ari."

Enjoy it for tonight, Tracey. Tomorrow you'll call it quits and leave.

She had to leave. His sanity couldn't afford to let her stay under his roof another night.

CHAPTER SIX

"I WAS TALKING ABOUT THE FUN of being in this farmhouse with you, Nikos. Just the two of us talking in the darkness together. I never had a brother or sister to share my room. Grandfather never allowed my friends to sleep over."

"What about those years when your father was alive?"

"We all lived at the mansion. Even with Daddy there to act as a buffer, we walked on eggshells."

"Yet that all changed when you took a husband and moved away." Every time Nikos thought about Tracey in bed with Karl, blackness enveloped him. "Surely he fulfilled your needs."

There was a long silence before she said, "My life with Karl was private."

His eyes closed tightly. "You mean behind closed doors where the press couldn't intrude."

"Yes."

"Ari told me your husband divorced you."

"That's true."

"If you loved him so much you married him the second you turned eighteen, then you must be in greater pain than I thought."

"I am…."

Nikos heard her pain and bit down so hard, he almost broke a tooth.

"Just so you know, I've never admitted that to anyone but you. I have another secret to tell."

Her comment made his breath catch in his lungs. "What is it?"

"Do you remember the time you came to the mansion with a gift for Samson?"

Nikos remembered every damn time when he'd hoped to be able to spend some time alone with her, and had the scars to prove it. "You'd just turned seventeen." Ari's age. Nikos had been playing a waiting game until she turned eighteen, then he'd planned to make his move.

"Yes. You'd brought my dog a new leash, and I told you he'd died of heartworm."

He had a premonition of what was coming,

and knew he wasn't going to like it. "Are you saying he didn't?"

"About two weeks after your previous visit, I found him dead on the grounds. I overheard two of the gardeners talking. They said my grandfather had killed Samson with a golf club, but no one else was ever to know."

Lord—

She had to clear her throat. "You should have seen him, Nikos. His dear little flat face all bloodied, his cute little sausage body, lifeless— I wanted to bury him in my favorite place, but the gardeners took him away. I had to pretend I didn't know in front of my grandfather."

Her sobs almost drove Nikos from the cot. He knew how much she'd loved that dog, and had to force himself not to get up and go over to comfort her.

"Th-That was his way of warning me not to cross him. Since that day I've been waiting for the time when I could get even.

"It would destroy him to see any of his money given to charity. But when I've won some of the board over to my side, I'm going to use it to do all kinds of good deeds."

What she'd told him had shaken him to the core. "Samson's gone to a better place."

"I know. That's the only thing that brings me comfort. Do you think he's with my parents?"

Her childlike question coming from her woman's body reached past his defenses. "Yes."

"But *how* do you know?"

That did it. He got out of bed and moved over to her side. Hunkering down he said, "I'm Helios, remember? I know everything."

Except that wasn't true. Nikos didn't know who the grown-up Tracey had turned into. Until he figured it out, he'd be like a madman chasing the source of the wind.

Exercising a control he didn't know he had, he undid the lid of her bottle.

"Here. You've cried so many tears, you need to replenish them."

A heartbreaking little laugh escaped. She put the bottle to her lips and drank until she'd emptied it.

"Ah," she said at last. "Ambrosia. The nectar of the gods. Thank you for listening to me. I had no idea all that was going to come out. Aren't you the luckiest man in the world to be stuck with me. But starting tomorrow, everything will be different. I promise."

So do I...

She was getting to him in ways faster than he could see them coming.

"Good night. Tracey."

"Good night, Nikos." She lay back down and turned away from him, making no attempt to prolong their good-night. He returned to his cot and drained his own bottle.

Two hours later he was still awake, consumed by uncontrollable jealousy over her feelings for Karl. It was one emotion he'd never felt in his life until now.

Tonight in her artless way, she'd completely disarmed him. Her depiction of life with her grandfather sounded like something out of the pages of an old crime family; his tight control on the women, the estate of armed guards in the guise of gardeners, the men who made up his board.

Divorced from her husband, Tracey was on her own with no protection from men like Vincent Morelli, who'd taken over the chairmanship of the board and was already warning her off. Now *there* was an ambitious man. Nikos didn't trust him.

Everything about the poor little rich girl was starting to make sense, except for one thing.

If her love for Karl was hopeless, then did it mean she was only after a rich husband as insurance for the future? Or did she truly mean to take her place on the board as a way to bury her pain?

Either answer caused a blackness to steal over him once more.

Tracey made certain she was up before Nikos. By the time he was awake and dressed, she'd eaten, and had coffee and rolls waiting for him.

She'd bought half a dozen pairs of jeans and T-shirts, her uniform from now on. With a sturdy pair of work boots, she felt prepared for her first day of farming.

"Let's go," Nikos said, getting up from the dining-room table. "The man hauling the tiller will be here in an hour. That gives us time to walk around your acre and place the flags."

They were wide red strips of cloth attached to sticks. Nikos had put all their farming tools on the back porch. "You'll need that mallet."

She picked it up along with a bundle of sticks.

He tucked a bundle under his strong arm. "Follow me."

At six in the morning, the temperature was bearable. From what she gathered, the Lazaridis farm took up a solid three-acre tract of land with the farmhouse sitting in the southwest corner near the main road.

For the next while Tracey walked in Nikos's footsteps. He put in the first marker with the mallet. Now she knew where the phrase *poetry in motion* came from.

It looked simple enough until it was her turn. She'd thought the pointed end of the stick would go right in. But she found the ground as unforgiving as Nikos had said. It took all her strength to penetrate the surface.

On her first attempt, the flag slanted and she had to start again. After five tries where she splintered some of the sticks and her nails, she made one more attempt, driving the mallet hard. Nikos told her it would do and walked on to the next spot.

By the time they'd walked the perimeter placing all the markers, perspiration had beaded her forehead and brows. Worse, her T-shirt stuck to her body, but she wouldn't give Nikos the satisfaction of knowing how dreadful she felt.

She excused herself for a minute and hurried inside the farmhouse to drink a ton of water. When she came back out, Nikos, who still looked fresh, was talking to a middle-aged man who'd driven up in a covered cab tractor. Behind him he hauled a big tiller.

After making the introductions, Nikos helped her up into the cab. "While I see about the irrigation, you sit on the instructor's seat and watch Elias. When you feel ready, then I'll drive with you and see how you do. Keep track of the time so you'll know how much to pay him for his hours and the rental."

"How much is a rental?"

"That's for you to find out. Ask all the questions you want. It's how you learn."

The next two hours proved to be an illuminating experience. Not in her whole life had she considered how grueling this kind of work could be. To think farmers did it with horses, or even worse, people, before there was machinery. Elias couldn't have been more patient as he answered her questions.

"You must have farmed all your life to perfect this skill."

He chuckled. "Now it's your turn."

"I'm terrified. What if I do something wrong and wreck everything?"

"It happens." He spread his arms.

With a groan, she got out of the cab and walked around to get in his seat. He took hers, then waited.

"Do what I did, then take us back to the farmhouse."

If she fouled up now…

No. She couldn't afford to think of failure.

"Okay. Here goes."

She turned on the motor and shifted the gears the way she'd seen him work them. But something went wrong and she discovered they were going backward instead of forward.

"Stop!" Elias cried.

Tracey did his bidding as fast as she could. He jumped down from the tractor. When she looked back, she could see the equipment had jackknifed.

After getting out herself, she was horrified to discover the force at that angle had broken off the hitch. She couldn't believe one wrong move had caused this much damage so fast!

Nikos was advancing on them with purpose in every long stride.

After the mistake over the cost of the seeds, why did this have to happen? Elias just stood there shaking his head.

She held her breath while Nikos inspected the mess and made a cell-phone call to someone. When he rang off he said, "You wait here for the tow truck. It's on its way now. I'll drive Elias back to town to get another tractor."

"I'm sorry, Nikos."

He eyed her narrowly. "This is your problem, not mine. Make sure you record the extra costs to bring another tractor out here. You'll also have to pay for the repairs, the tow truck and overtime pay for Elias. He had another job to do later today. Now he'll have to cancel in order to finish the one here."

She turned to the other man. "I got the gear position mixed up. Next time I'll do it right. I promise."

Elias nodded before following Nikos to the truck. With a sinking heart, Tracey watched them drive away. She was such a miserable failure, Nikos didn't even bother to point it out. He didn't have to. The proof was staring her in the face.

By the time she'd gone into the farmhouse for more water, the tow truck had arrived and taken the tractor away. She'd barely had time to make more notations in the ledger when the sound of another tractor reached her ears. She hurried outside, but there was no sign of the truck.

"Let us start again," Elias said, motioning for her to climb in the driver's seat now that he'd hooked up the tiller to the hitch.

"I know what I did wrong. This time I'll do it right. Show me the gear positions again."

As determined as she'd ever been in her life, she started the motor and miracle of miracles the tractor crept forward. The trick now was to stay in the grooves.

She kept looking over her shoulder, satisfied to see the tiller was turning the soil. Sometimes it tugged and threw her off-kilter. Eventually she'd covered the whole acre. On the way back she veered off course and came to a stop short of the spot where Nikos stood watching.

He'd returned from town. Another man from the company had followed him in a truck to hook up the tiller and take Elias home.

The three men appeared to share a private joke

in Greek before Nikos walked over to her. She wiped her face with the sides of her arms. She was dripping with perspiration. Their eyes met. His gleamed with a strange light.

"Take us over the ground one more time between the markers and then it will be ready for tomorrow."

Did he mean now? Right this minute? Tracey smothered a moan. She didn't dare slow down in front of him, but she didn't know where she was going to find the strength in this heat.

"Are you sure you dare?" she teased in an effort to pretend nothing was wrong.

"I've always been a risk taker."

"You've never driven with me."

His brows furrowed. "How many Ferraris did you go through?"

"You mean besides the Lagondas?" she snapped. "I've lost count." Karl was the one who'd loved fast cars, but she could save the explanation because Nikos wouldn't buy any of it.

Concentrate on the job at hand, Tracey. Don't let Nikos find anything to fault.

Running on sheer will power and adrenaline, she turned on the motor. There were many hits and misses, hiccups and burps along the way, but after another hour had passed, she drew up to the back of the house and shut off the motor, utterly drained. But at least they were back in one piece and the equipment hadn't been ruined.

Nikos flashed her an oblique glance. "One day you'll be sitting in a board meeting and someone will complain about the cost of new machinery. They'll insist it's a waste of money. That's when you'll remember this day.

"Think how frustrating it would have been if the tractor or the tiller had broken down and you had to send for new parts. It's vital to have state-of-the-art equipment that works the first time, especially with an inexperienced driver."

She'd been waiting for that salvo and he hadn't disappointed her.

"Unnecessary delays and costly repairs of ancient machinery drive up the price, which can put your company's books in the red."

Tracey understood what he was saying, but for the life of her she felt too weak and dehydrated in this heat to talk.

"In the morning Elias will come to show you how to pack the ground."

She nodded, but it was doubtful she'd be alive by evening, never mind tomorrow. Feeling distinctly light-headed, she made it into the house and went into the bathroom where she drank from the cold tap.

Tomorrow she'd be smart and leave several changes of clothes in here so she could shower whenever she came in and change clothes. Still clinging to the sink for support, she heard a knock on the door.

"Yes?"

"What's taking you so long?"

"Oh—I—I'm sorry." Her head was swimming. She was almost afraid to let go of the sink.

"Are you all right?"

Was that concern she heard in Nikos's voice? She couldn't believe it.

"Of course."

"I've left your suitcase outside the door in case you wanted to shower."

"Thank you."

"Your lunch is ready."

"I'll be right out."

She waited until he left, then opened the door and grabbed her suitcase. Yet she couldn't summon the strength to shower. A strange lethargy had taken over her senses. She left everything there and walked through the house, aware she was ready to pass out if she didn't eat.

Nikos took one look at her and to her surprise, helped her into one of the chairs. He'd made sandwiches and fruit. She devoured everything without saying anything. When she checked her watch, it was two o'clock. No wonder she felt so enervated.

"You should have eaten more breakfast," Nikos admonished her in a low tone.

"I agree."

"Tomorrow you'll take water with you. No caffeine for breakfast."

"Understood."

His eyes held a bleak expression. "I should have remembered a redhead has more trouble handling this heat. I want you to lie down."

"I'll be fine."

"Mind me, Tracey."

He meant business. In her fragile state, she had no desire to fight him.

It felt so good to stretch out on her cot, she moaned loud enough that Nikos heard her. He brought her a cold bottle of water from the fridge.

"Thank you. Please don't do the dishes or the washing. I'll get up in a little while and take care of things."

He ignored her and set up the fan so it blew on her face.

"That feels good."

"It's supposed to."

"You make a terrific nurse."

"Then be a terrific patient and stay there."

"Okay."

"You've got heat prostration."

She'd heard of it, but had never suffered from it. Darting him a furtive glance, she noticed he'd brought in one of the chairs and sat near her, working with his laptop.

"You don't have to babysit me."

His intense gaze fastened on her. "Stop talking and rest."

"I'm all right. Really."

"We'll see. Go to sleep."

"How did I do today?" Her speech sounded slurred. She was already half gone and closed her eyes.

Nikos didn't like her pallor. He felt her forehead. She was burning up and didn't respond to his touch. He wrapped her head of damp red tendrils in a cold wet towel, then got on his cell phone to Kalambaka.

"This is Nikos Lazaridis. I need an ambulance sent immediately to the farm for a Tracey Conner. She could have heatstroke."

"They're on their way, *Kyrie* Lazaridis."

He hung up and went into the bathroom to gather some things in her suitcase. Before long the paramedics arrived and loaded her in the ambulance, hooking her up to an IV.

Dear Lord. If anything happened to her—

Elias had said something about her looking pale. But Nikos had been so bent on driving her away from the farm, he'd dismissed the other man's observation, thinking Elias was just another man smitten by her charms.

Nikos followed the ambulance in his truck and raced into the hospital. The staff placed her on a gurney and rolled her into one of the cubicles in the ER where the attending physician took over.

"It was my fault she was out in the heat too long today. Whatever you have to do to keep her alive, do it!" he ordered the doctor.

The older man eyed him calmly. "Heatstroke

is serious, but don't borrow trouble. We'll do everything we can to keep her organs from shutting down. Does she have a relative we can phone to inform and get information?"

Only her ex-husband, who'd apparently wanted his freedom from her. That was something Nikos couldn't comprehend. In fact it didn't make sense.

"No," he bit out. "I'll take care of it, and the charges."

"Then I suggest you go to the reception area and give the clerk the particulars. One of the staff will let you know when you can see her."

An hour passed. Not even the death of his parents had affected him to this degree. This was his fault. The mere thought of Tracey not being alive somewhere on this earth was anathema to him.

When he couldn't stand the waiting any longer, he walked through the room to the curtained cubicle. The doctor was just coming out.

"Is she awake?"

"Not yet, but we've got her stabilized. I'm sending her to a private room. If you want to go on up to 340 West, she'll be arriving shortly."

Nikos took the stairs two at a time to the third floor. He reached the room five minutes ahead of her. When they wheeled her in, she looked so fragile it was all he could do not to reach over and hold her in his arms the way he'd wanted to do years ago outside the mansion.

But this time Nikos had been the one to put her in danger, not her grandfather. If Leon knew the truth, he'd tell Nikos he was a bastard, and he'd be right.

Nikos had been so intent on punishing her because he thought she was a desperate heiress playing a part to make him her husband, he'd put her life in jeopardy. A cold sweat broke out on his body when he thought of her not coming out of this.

Don't die on me, Tracey.

The staff hooked her up to several monitors. He was finally allowed to pull a chair next to her.

"Her vitals are better," the nurse informed him.

"Thank God."

"I'll be back."

Relieved to be alone with her at last, he whispered, "Tracey? Can you hear me? It's Nikos."

She was making restless movements. Her

eyelids twitched, and her lips seemed to be trying to form words. Nikos heard moaning sounds. She had to be dreaming.

He jumped up from the chair and leaned over her. "Wake up, Tracey."

"Don't send me away," she murmured.

"I wouldn't do that."

She thrashed around. "Hide me—"

He swallowed hard. Her movements were frantic. "Come on, Tracey. Wake up," he said urgently.

"Don't send me back— I'd rather die first—"

He cupped her soft cheek with his palm. "You're not going anywhere. It's just a bad dream."

Suddenly her eyes opened. Those gorgeous turquoise eyes were filled with terror. "Don't send me back to him, Nikos."

Him?

Her grandfather was dead. Who was she afraid of? Her ex-husband? That didn't compute, not if she was still in love with him.

But what if she wasn't...

Nikos's heart leaped. What if she was carrying another secret she hadn't been able to tell him last night.

Was Von Axel the real reason she'd come to Nikos? Because she needed protection from him?

"I won't let anyone hurt you," he promised, smoothing the damp red curls off her forehead.

"Nikos?" Finally she said his name with recognition. She tried to lift her head off the mattress. "What happened? Where am I?"

"In the hospital. You've had heatstroke, but you're going to be fine now. Thank God I got you here in time."

Tears welled in the corners of her eyes. "Some farmer I make."

"Hush, Tracey. I don't know anyone who did a finer job on her first day than you. Elias is in awe of you. So am I," he admitted proudly.

She shook her head. "You're making that up, but I promise that from now on I'll do exactly as you say. What good is state-of-the-art machinery if the woman operating it is the cause for all the delays?"

Tracey—

Nikos lowered his head and brushed her lips with his own. They felt cool. A shudder shook his body to remember how hot she'd felt a few hours earlier.

Looking down at her he said, "Bringing you to the farm was a mistake."

"No it wasn't—" She tried to raise herself up again. "I promise I'll improve. You have to give me a little more time."

He gently eased her back. "No one could do better, but this heat is too much for someone not used to it."

She reached out to grab his arm. "Please don't tell me I have to leave the farm. I've been looking forward to the planting. Ever since we flew over those crops the other day, I've been imagining mine."

Nikos couldn't lie to himself any longer. The pleading in her eyes and voice told him this was no act on her part. Whatever else he might think of her, she was putting her heart into this project. And she was frightened. Whether of Karl or another man, Nikos intended to find out.

His hand covered hers. "Listen to me, Tracey. The farmhouse doesn't give you enough relief from the sun."

"What if I do my job in increments? Say two hours a day, then spend the rest of the time inside."

"No."

He never wanted to live through an experience like this again.

"Then let me stay in an air-conditioned hotel in town. I'll buy a car with good air-conditioning and drive out to the farm every morning. When I feel the heat getting to me, I'll quit and drive back to town to cool off. What hotel would you suggest I check into?"

When he became aware he was squeezing her hand, he let it go. How ironic that as late as this afternoon, he'd hoped she'd be gone from the farm by tonight. Yet now that she'd proposed a plan to do just that, he found himself fighting it.

He drew in a ragged breath. "There's only one with the kind of air-conditioning you're used to."

"Would you hate it if I stayed at your brother's hotel?"

Evidently Ari had told her about his father's business.

Yes, Nikos would hate it. But not because of his brother. In just a few days she'd made her presence felt at the farmhouse. He was very much afraid it was an indelible one....

"I think you need to sleep on any decisions."

"I've been asleep. Now I'm wide awake and

want to leave the hospital." She sat up and moved her legs over the side of the bed.

Her hospital gown had ridden up her elegant legs to her thighs. He tried not to look at them. It was a losing battle.

"The doctor says you have to stay overnight."

"But I feel normal. If you told him that when I leave here I'm going straight to a cold hotel room where there's room service, I'm sure he'd give orders for my release."

That was what Nikos was afraid of. Then he wouldn't have the rest of the night to be alone with her. Dropping in to the hotel to see her, coming in and out the doors in full view of his family, wasn't the same thing as camping out together with no else around.

She'd told Nikos it was fun.

It had been fun for him, too. More fun than he'd had in his whole life with a woman.

She's nice, Uncle Nikos. Funny, too.

The Tracey he'd once known was both those things. And much more… A long time ago she'd planned a picnic for the two of them. One that had rebounded on her in ways he didn't want to think about, and all because of Nikos.

In frustration he raked a bronzed hand through his hair.

"We'll see what he says when he looks in on you later. Here's some juice. The nurse said to drink as much as you can."

"Yes, Doctor."

She accepted the cup with a meekness that was pure pretense. Only then did she seem to notice her bare limbs and cover them with the bed sheet. A delicate flush filled her cheeks, indicating an innate modesty that surprised him considering her wild behavior in public.

The duality in her nature was driving him crazy.

Worse, her gorgeous coloring tortured him.

The nameless, faceless man who'd frightened her in her dream had become Nikos's adversary. One day soon he'd get what he wanted out of her and make certain she was never bothered again.

"You're looking a little fierce, Nikos. I don't blame you. If you'd rather I stayed in the hospital overnight so you can spend some uninterrupted time alone, it's fine with me. Honestly."

Tracey's sincerity wrapped around him like a silken cord.

"After what happened to you, you're my first priority."

"You mean your liability," she teased.

After putting the empty cup on the bed table, she lay down with her back toward him. "Go away. You've done all you can for me. I'm in a hospital safe and sound now."

Brave words for a woman with an enemy. But not for long…

CHAPTER SEVEN

THE MEDIUM-SIZE FOUR-STAR Thessaly Hotel built in neoclassic lines had every amenity. Tracey found her room on the second floor; it was lovely. The balcony looked out on a view of the city and the Meteora.

Nikos's family couldn't have been more accommodating. Leon, who was forty and strongly resembled Nikos in height and coloring, had met them in the foyer.

"When my brother called to tell me he was coming home to Kalambaka, he didn't let on he was bringing someone with him. Welcome to the Thessaly Hotel, Ms. Loretto. It's our privilege to have you here."

"Thank you, Mr. Lazaridis."

"Call me Leon."

"She goes by her maiden name of Conner, Papa, and prefers to be called Tracey."

His golden-brown eyes had darted to Ari in surprise. "Is that so, my son?" His slightly mocking tone had reminded her so much of Nikos right then she couldn't believe it.

The younger man had grinned. "If you want anything, Tracey, I'm at your service."

Tracey had caught a silent exchange between Leon and Nikos. If there was tension between the brothers, she didn't feel it.

"Tracey's just out of the hospital," Nikos had reminded everyone, slipping a strong arm around her waist. She'd knew he'd done it out of concern for her physical well-being, but she wished it had been for a different reason. "Let's get her to her room."

"Right this way," both Leon and his son had said at the same time. She thought Nikos would find it funny. But he'd remained sober faced as the four of them had entered the elevator.

Once upstairs in her room, Nikos introduced her to his sister-in-law, Maria, and his niece, Irenà.

They were both charming and had been preparing things, trying to anticipate Tracey's every need. She was very touched.

"How old are you, Irena?"

"Fifteen."

"That's how old I was when I first met your uncle Nikos."

Irena smiled and sat on the end of the queen-size bed. "Where was that?"

"At my house in Buffalo, New York."

"It's big, huh?"

Tracey's eyes met Nikos's before she said, "Too big."

"Try three hundred rooms, Irena," her uncle informed everyone.

Ari whistled, and shook his fingers in a typical Greek gesture.

"Actually Nikos and I met outside the mansion. He was holding my dog."

"What kind is it?"

"Samson was a pug."

"Oh, they are so cute."

Avoiding Nikos's eyes, Tracey nodded, giving herself time to clear her throat. "My grandfather had brought Nikos home as a guest. He'd already told me about your uncle, whom he likened to the Greek god Helios for whom the Colossus had been erected at Rhodes.

"Being a fanciful girl with my head in the clouds, the second I saw Nikos I thought he was Helios come to life!"

The whole room burst into laughter, except Nikos, who only smiled from one corner of his mouth. But that look turned her heart over.

"My uncle's not quite that big," Irena said, beaming at him.

"My grandfather was scared of him."

"Of Uncle Nikos?"

"Yes."

"Why?"

"Because he's so smart. Grandfather said Nikos knew more than he did. If you'd known my grandfather, you would understand what an astounding thing that had been for him to say."

"Have you ever been scared of our uncle?" Ari asked with a grin.

"All the time."

That brought the house down.

While the others fussed over her, making her feel like visiting royalty, she refused to look at Nikos.

Although she could wish she were back at the

farmhouse, she wasn't about to complain. Nikos was on the verge of calling off the whole project. One wrong move from her and he'd tell her his original plan to help her wasn't going to work after all.

In the hospital, she'd made up her mind that from here on out, she would do whatever he told her without question.

The dreams of becoming his wife one day had been nothing more than vain imaginings of a naive young girl. But now that she was a woman, she could learn invaluable lessons from him, and didn't dare jeopardize this precious time he was giving her without thought of recompense.

"Tracey needs her sleep," Maria announced. "I'll watch out for her tonight, Nikos."

He pulled his cell phone from his pocket. "What's your number, Tracey?"

When she gave it to him, he programmed it, then leveled his gaze on her. "Where's your cell phone?"

"In my purse on the table."

"Did you bring the charger with you?"

"Yes. It's in there, too."

"You'll need an adaptor."

"I'll get her one out of the office," Ari volunteered and left the room like a shot.

Without her permission, Nikos opened the bag and reached for her phone. "Do you have any of the digits programmed?"

"Yes. Numbers one and two." Sadie, the housekeeper at the mansion, could be reached on one. The other number was Karl's.

Nikos held her gaze for a tension-filled moment as if reading her mind before he said, "I'll program it so you can call me on three, or Maria on four."

Seconds later he handed the phone to her. "Try phoning me."

She did his bidding and heard his cell ring.

"Good. Now call Maria."

Nikos was nothing if not thorough, but after she'd passed out on him, she couldn't blame him for taking extra precautions.

Once she'd pressed the fourth digit and heard his sister-in-law's phone ring inside the pocket of the other woman's dress, his tall rigid body appeared to relax somewhat.

He pulled the charger out of her purse. "I'll be over in the morning. We'll talk about our plans at breakfast."

Her eyes sought his in a searching glance. "I'll look forward to it, Nikos. Thank you for getting me to the hospital in time. You'll never have to worry about me overheating again. I swear it."

A nerve throbbed at the corner of his male mouth. "I believe you."

"Okay," Maria spoke up, waving her arms. "Everyone out. Shoo!"

As good-nights were being said, Ari came back in the room and plugged the adaptor into the wall plug near her bed.

"Thanks, Ari."

"You're welcome. I'll set it up."

"That's all right," Nikos said, taking charge. Tracey thought she saw a flash of impatience in those golden eyes.

Ari shrugged. "Sure."

Maria took the phone from Nikos. "*I'll* take care of Tracey." She spoke with authority, like a mother who'd decided to break up any trouble before it could start.

Tracey struggled to keep a straight face. She doubted that any other person in the world could get away with telling Nikos what to do.

"I'll see you at nine. *Kalinihta,* Tracey."

He'd never said anything to her in Greek before. For some reason it sounded intimate, as if they had a special connection. A weakness attacked her body.

"*Kalinihta*, Nikos. Good night."

He left the room behind the other members of the family, no doubt eager to do something exciting with the rest of his night. If Tracey thought about where he might be headed, she'd go mad.

The second the door closed, Maria put the end of the charger in Tracey's phone and set it on her bedside table. "Nikos brought up your suitcase." She opened it. "What can I get for you?"

"The peignoir? My nightgown is back at the farmhouse in the bathroom, waiting to be washed I'm sorry to say."

Maria shook her head. "I can't imagine what Nikos was thinking when he took you out to that awful place." She handed the robe to Tracey. "When Ari told us you were living there, I couldn't believe it.

"Of course it has special meaning for Nikos and Leon, but it's not a fit place to live anymore."

Tracey wasn't sure how much to reveal. "I

believe he has plans for it." At this point she didn't want to talk about it.

"That's good, but in the meantime you stay here. Let him play soldier boy by himself." The expression struck Tracey funny and she started to laugh. Maria laughed with her, bonding them on a deeper level. "That's what he and Leon used to play when they were little."

"Ari called it an outpost."

They were still laughing when her phone rang. Only one person would phone her at this time of night. She reached for it without checking the caller ID.

"Karl? Forgive me for not calling you yet, but I—"

"This isn't your ex-husband."

The deep male voice she'd know anywhere had just cut her off. Her body started to tremble. "Nikos—"

"Are you alone?"

"No."

Maria eyed her curiously.

"Your sister-in-law and I were just talking."

"You're supposed to be in bed."

"I'm going."

"See that you do."

"You need a good night's sleep, too. Promise me you won't do any work. I'll take care of everything when I'm out there tomorrow. When you do go home, drive safely."

"Tracey—"

Her heart skipped an extra beat. He sounded anxious. She guessed he was worried she might end up back in the hospital. "Yes?"

"Nothing. Sleep well."

When she hung up and turned around, Maria had gone.

Finally alone, she got ready for bed and slid under the covers. The air-conditioning was so efficient, she burrowed underneath.

But as luxurious as her bed was, she missed her cot that tipped if she didn't move the right way. She craved the scent of Nikos after he came out of the shower and the fan blew it through the warm air in her direction.

No more water bottles by her bed. No more talks in the night. Those had been the greatest times of her life.

She ached for him.

If she didn't know his future plans were

already mapped out, she would phone him back just to hear his voice again.

Still wide awake, she reached for the phone and listened to her messages.

She'd been putting off returning calls. Now there were ten of them, one each from David and Vincent. She had nothing to say to them. Their day would come when she showed up at her first board meeting.

There were two calls from Sadie over domestic problems that could wait until tomorrow. Karl accounted for the other six, all of them a potential emergency.

His lover of eight years had broken up with him. Not even the divorce seemed to be helping them get back together.

She decided she'd better phone him. He picked up on the third ring.

"Tracey—you have no idea how much I needed to hear from you."

"I'm sorry I haven't phoned before now, Karl. I've been busy."

"Where are you?"

"It doesn't matter. Tell me what's wrong."

"My whole life's falling apart. Could you come

to Montreux and help me? I'm staying at the Vaudois Palace."

"For how long?"

"While my luck at the gambling tables still holds."

He usually won. His winnings managed to keep him afloat. When they didn't, she put funds in his account.

"Tell you what. Give me a few more days and then—Karl? I've got another call on the line. Hold on."

She had to roll over to turn on the bedside lamp. Then she checked the caller ID.

Nikos! Again?

"Karl? I have to take this. I'll phone you right back."

"Promise?"

"Wait for my call!"

Tracey double clicked, but it was too late. Nikos had hung up. She pressed the speed dial. It rang half a dozen times before he clicked on.

"Nikos?"

"If I wakened you, I'm sorry, Tracey," he said without preamble.

"You didn't. I couldn't reach the phone in time." It was better he thought she'd been resting.

"How are you feeling? The truth!"

"I'm fine." *Now that you've called.*

"I wanted you to know that when I drove up to the farmhouse just now I found a sack at the door with your name on it."

That meant Nikos had gone straight back to the farm. She shouldn't be happy about it, but she was.

"Who on earth would leave a present for me? No one knows where I am. Did you open it?"

"It's not for me."

He hadn't asked if he could look in her purse, but he'd been so upset at the time she'd understood why. This was different.

"Everything I have is yours. Isn't that what you told me the other night at your condo? Go ahead and see what's inside."

She could hear rustling sounds and counted the seconds until he spoke into the phone.

"It's a broad-rimmed straw hat for farming. There's a note. It's from…Ari." The surprise in his voice echoed hers.

"You're kidding—what did he write?"

"This is to protect your flawless complexion.

Did I tell you your hair shines like a newly minted American penny? Your eyes take me to the South Seas. I could swim in them. How about dinner tomorrow night? My treat. Ari."

"How sweet of him."

After a silence, Nikos said, "He's got a major crush on you."

She chuckled. "If I were five years younger…"

"The problem is, he doesn't care that you're seven years older. In fact with your history, that makes you vastly more tempting."

Tears stung her eyes. For a little while she'd forgotten.

"Why don't you say what's really on your mind, Nikos? That I'm the kind of baggage you don't want near your nephew. Don't worry. I won't encourage him. In fact, I wouldn't dream of it. I'm here to learn about farming.

"Let me know in the morning if you've changed your mind about teaching me, and I'll leave Greece. I have to tell you it's getting harder and harder to be your personal punching bag. Now if there isn't anything else on your mind, I'd like to go to sleep."

She clicked off before she said something

worse, then phoned Karl again. It was the only way not to break down sobbing.

"Karl? I'm back. Tomorrow I'll make arrangements to come. The minute I know my plans, I'll let you know when I'll be arriving."

"I can always count on you. Thanks, Tracey."

"You're welcome. Now I've got to go to sleep."

"I wish *I* could. Sweet dreams."

Sweet dreams? What were those? She hung up, dying inside.

Everything had gone wrong. Her attempts to learn farming had ended in humiliating failure. What a fool she'd been to have stayed out in the heat so long, Nikos had been forced to get her to the hospital.

Pride goeth before the fall.

His family had been wonderful to her, but she'd put everyone out. It was all her fault. She'd wanted to follow through with this business arrangement and make her presence felt on the board one day, but it seemed as if she'd become a walking disaster.

To make matters worse, she was so in love with Nikos she was in danger of telling him.

He was already disgusted with her on several

levels. All he would need to hear was a confession of her deepest feelings for him, and the nightmare she'd had in the hospital would become a reality. She could still remember Nikos's brutal rejection of her in such vivid detail, moisture bathed her face.

Trying to pull herself together, she set her wrist alarm for seven and lay back down, wondering how she was going to function from here on out. After Nikos's warning to leave Ari alone, she knew she couldn't take much more.

What she and Nikos needed was a break from each other, the sooner the better. As soon as she'd spent a couple of hours helping do the seedbed packing tomorrow, she'd announce she was taking a brief trip and would be back within twenty-four hours.

Relieved to have a plan that would put some needed space between them, she finally fell asleep. When morning came she showered and dressed in clean jeans and a white T-shirt. After availing herself of the fruit and juice in her room, she slipped out the back entrance of the hotel without anyone seeing her.

Once she'd walked a few blocks along the main

street, she hailed a taxi and asked the driver to take her to a car dealership.

The doors didn't open until eight o'clock. While she waited, she made all her flight arrangements to Switzerland. At five to eight, an attractive-looking guy close to her age with dark brown hair and eyes arrived and opened up the dealership.

Since she was the only client, he gave her his undivided attention. His name was Dimitri. Apparently his father owned the place.

Tracey didn't think he recognized her, but he did flirt with her. Not so outrageously that he turned her off. Just enough to keep her smiling.

He helped her pick out a new blue compact car. She paid for it with a credit card that still bore the name Tracey Loretto. When she signed the paperwork, she put her temporary address as the Thessaly Hotel. She took care not to mention Nikos or his family.

By eight-fifteen she was ready to leave the bay where the mechanic had filled her car with gas. Dimitri asked if he could take her out for dinner one night soon. She told him she was too busy, then thanked him for his help and whizzed away.

Already she needed the air-conditioning which worked like a charm. Ten minutes later, she pulled up to the farm, where she expected to see Elias ready to go to work. But there was no equipment in sight, only Nikos's truck.

After yesterday he probably needed to sleep in and had told the older man to come later in the day.

Pleased Nikos was still here, she pulled up behind the truck and got out. She would fix them a big breakfast. This way he didn't have to drive into town. It would save time all the way around.

She knocked on the front door, her heart fluttering in anticipation of what he would say when he saw her standing on the other side. When he didn't come, she knocked harder. Still no answer. He was probably in a deep sleep.

The only thing to do was phone him, but she hated waking him.

Of course he'd locked up for the night, but something made her try the handle anyway. To her surprise, it gave. The door swung open, giving her a view of his unmade bed. He had to be in the bathroom.

She closed the door behind herself and walked through the living room to the kitchen. As she opened the fridge and reached for the eggs, she saw movement out of the corner of her eye.

It was Nikos drying himself off with a towel. Their eyes met for an instant.

Her surprise was so great, the carton fell to the floor, causing it to open. The eggs splattered on the old linoleum.

Acting as if this were an everyday occurrence, he calmly hitched the towel around his hips.

"*Kalimera,* Tracey."

"Good morning," she whispered shakily.

"How did you get here?"

"I bought a car this morning."

"I see."

She could hardly concentrate on what he'd said because he was moving toward her with purpose. She ended up flattening herself against the closed refrigerator door.

He came to stand in front of her, enveloping her in his body warmth, though they weren't quite touching.

His eyes wandered over each feature of her face lifted to his gaze, until it reached her eyes. "Ari was right about everything, but I have a much better idea than swimming in those aqua-blue depths."

So saying, he put his strong arms around her, pulling her up against him so her feet left the floor. With her body pinned between his well-defined chest and the fridge, his dark head descended, then his compelling mouth was covering hers.

At the first touch of his lips, coherent thought fled.

"Nikos—" She gasped at the indescribable feel of their bodies melded to each other. Heat against heat, setting off an explosion of rapture inside her so great, she thought she would faint.

Her avid red mouth couldn't get enough of his. The more he sought, the more she helped him find. Then she became the one seeking, restlessly covering his face and neck with kisses.

Back and forth they gave and kept on giving, each kiss becoming longer, deeper, until her body trembled with desire she couldn't contain. Tracey's hunger for him was reaching critical mass.

Her red head fell back on the graceful column of her neck. "I've dreamed of this for so long. Love me, Nikos—" she begged, intoxicated by the passion he'd aroused with his mouth and body.

"I intend to," came his husky response.

His arm went behind her knees and he started carrying her into the living room. She slid her arms around his neck, pressing urgent kisses to his mouth and jaw.

Feverish in her need of him now, she scarcely felt him lower her to the cot. Not wanting any air between them, she pulled him down to her, not willing to give up any part of him.

That was when the cot gave out and hit the floor with a thud. Nikos landed on top of her.

"Oh—"

He rolled off her onto the linoleum. "Did I hurt you, Tracey?"

She shook her head, laughing helplessly at what had just happened. "I wish I had a picture of you like this." What a sight he made, barely draped at this point. "I'd call it, 'Colossus toppled.'"

His lips twitched. "That's very appropriate considering it was a woman who caused his downfall."

A shaft of pain entered her heart. "But not the right woman." Nikos had his plans…the spell was broken.

Tracey sat up and covered him with the blanket before getting to her feet. She looked down at those eyes of gold staring up at her.

"I was asking for this when I walked in here. As you told me on the yacht, I'm Tracey Loretto in your eyes, no Tracey Connor. A woman who barges her way in unannounced and uninvited.

"I could deny that I planned for any of this to happen this morning. But maybe subconsciously I hoped it would, if only to bring closure to the crush I once had on you.

"Grandfather made certain he ruined my picnic that day. Looking back, it saved me from making an even greater fool of myself because I definitely had plans to seduce you in the rose garden.

"Don't ever let anyone tell you that a teenager can't lust after an older man. I wanted you on any terms the first time I laid eyes on you.

"Between your visits, I dreamed of all the ways I would make love to you. I lived in anticipation of all the ways you would make love to me that I didn't know about yet because I didn't have the experience.

"Every time you came to the mansion and I heard your voice, I could hardly breathe. You were the man I wanted to make me into a woman, but things didn't turn out the way I planned. In fact my initiation into womanhood was so drastically different than anything I could have conceived, I can't believe I survived it."

"Then you're not in love with Karl."

She averted his eyes. "I care about him."

But she didn't love Von Axel. Nikos knew it!

Tears crept into her voice. "The tabloids have exploited everything they could learn about my life, but you're the only one who knows the sordid secrets of a young girl's heart.

"Now if you'll excuse me, I'm going to clean up the mess I made in the kitchen. Breakfast should be ready in five minutes. I need to talk to you about something important."

Nikos watched her leave the living room. He didn't know how long he lay there in a daze before getting up. At some point, he pulled clean clothes from the chest of drawers and dressed without conscious thought.

In one short half hour he'd lived, and died. Anything else in his thirty-eight years before this didn't count.

"Nikos? Breakfast is on the table!"

He felt her eyes on him as he entered the dining room and sat down. "I managed to salvage four eggs, so I turned them into an omelet." She'd made coffee and had supplied rolls and fruit. He couldn't fault her for anything.

"The eggs are perfect."

"Thank you. They taste good to me, too."

His gaze played over her. No one seeing this composed woman pouring him coffee would guess how she'd burst into flame in his arms a little while ago. With her body, her mouth, her hands, she'd set off a conflagration in him so white-hot and crackling, he was a changed man.

After what she'd revealed from the depths of her soul, he didn't want to hurt her. Never again.

But he had questions. If it took him the rest of his life to get the answers, then so be it.

"What did you want to talk to me about?"

"Isn't Elias coming today?"

"No. I asked him to wait until tomorrow so you'd have a day to rest from the heat."

"Thank you. Under the circumstances, do you think you could ask him to wait until the day after tomorrow?"

Nikos sensed something was coming he wouldn't like. "If you need that much time to recover, of course."

"It won't hurt the ground? I mean, we won't have to till it one more time if we wait?"

Like the question she'd asked about farming at night, his inclination to laugh was tempered by her earnestness because she really didn't know.

He shook his head. "Another day won't matter."

"Good." She suddenly averted her eyes. "I need to fly to Switzerland. It will be a short trip. I'll be back by tomorrow night."

His hand closed around the juice glass so hard, some of it spilled. He had the gut feeling she was going to see her ex-husband. What kind of a hold did that monster have on her?

"I'll take you."

Her head flew back. She stared at him as if she'd never seen him before. "I should think you have other things to do with your free time. This is something I need to take care of myself."

"After just being released from the hospital, I won't let you go alone."

"After the way I lost control a few minutes ago, I think you can see I'm fully recovered. As it is, I'm mortified over what just happened."

"You mean what *didn't* happen," he reminded her.

"Only because of the cot."

"We had the floor, but you left me lying there. Don't start flailing yourself needlessly. After living in such close proximity, it was bound to happen. I could have kept my distance when I saw you in the kitchen."

The nerve throbbing at the base of her throat fascinated him.

"What are you saying, Nikos?"

"I think you know. With your grandfather acting as watchdog, I wouldn't have made repeat visits to the mansion if I hadn't been attracted to you, too."

She bit her lip. "I hoped that was true, but then the visits stopped."

He studied her through his lashes. "You got married."

A bleakness entered her eyes. "I thought you might have come one more time."

"Before the wedding, you mean?"

"Yes," she whispered.

"I offered to host a prenuptial party for you in Buffalo. Your grandfather said thanks, but… no thanks."

Losing some of her color, Tracey pushed herself

away from the table and stood up. "I wish I'd known—" she cried. "How did he dare do that?"

"Because he sensed something between you and me, and didn't want me influencing you at the last second."

She hugged her arms to her waist as if she were in great physical pain, yet unwilling to let it out in front of him.

"Since that time I'm afraid you and I have sustained a consuming curiosity over forbidden fruit, Tracey. This morning we were able to satisfy our desire to taste it. I for one found it all the sweeter for the waiting."

"It was sweet to me, too," she admitted with stunning honesty. "I can't even imagine what it would have tasted like if Grandfather hadn't interfered. But it wasn't sweet enough for you to pull me back down on the floor and kiss us both into oblivion just now.

"That's because I'm Tracey Loretto, and too much has happened we can't ignore. We're not the same people anymore, and I can't go back to my innocence."

There was a tragic quality in her tone that cut him up inside.

"No one can. The thing to do now is persevere in the desire to make your mark on the Loretto board. I'd like to see you do it. So while we're not farming, I'll show you how to study the latest company reports and make sense of them. We'll get started while we're in flight."

She stared at him. "If you're sure this won't interfere with your plans. When I asked you to help me, I didn't intend that you be with me on a twenty-four hour basis."

A wealth of emotions, guilty and otherwise, were eating him alive. All these years he'd been lying to himself about his inability to get along with Leon. It wasn't his brother who'd kept him away so long. He hadn't wanted to come home without bringing Tracey with him.

When she'd married Karl, it had been the death of his dreams. Then she'd appeared on the Padakis yacht, turning his world inside out once again. This time he hadn't let her get away.

"Let me decide what I want."

"I've been a nuisance, but after I get back from seeing Karl, you'll notice a difference in me."

Nikos closed his eyes tightly for a moment. "If

you're divorced, why would you ever want to be with him again?"

She sucked in her breath. "Some divorces aren't that cut and dried. He's having problems."

"You feel sorry for him?"

"In a way. When he hurts, *I* hurt."

What in the hell? Nikos knew he wasn't mistaken about the terrifying man in her nightmare. As for her breathtaking response to Nikos before the cot had broken…

"Where in Switzerland are you meeting him?"

"Montreux. I'm already booked at the Vaudois Palace."

Under Von Axel's name?

"Since I'm going with you, I'll book us a suite. We'll fly to Geneva and take a helicopter from there. The hotel has its own landing pad. That makes it convenient."

If her ex thought he could take advantage of her feelings to spend the night with him for old times' sake, he could think again.

"I don't have my suitcase here."

"We'll buy you what you need when we reach the hotel and take him to dinner."

She hesitated, as if she were on the verge of

telling him that wasn't part of her plan. But then she surprised him by nodding and started to clear the table.

He got up and took the rest of the things into the kitchen. "I'll send for the helicopter. It should be here within a half hour."

The Tracey beneath his roof was not the shallow, wanton heiress he'd accused her of being in his heart. At her core she was the same sweet girl he'd first met, but terrible things had altered the woman she'd become. He wouldn't rest until he found out all her secrets and made her world safe.

CHAPTER EIGHT

THE ELEGANT VAUDOIS PALACE, the jewel of the Swiss Riviera, looked out over the shimmering blue waters of Lake Geneva. Tracey had been here several times with Karl, who enjoyed its sophisticated ambience. Yet if she could be anywhere in the world, she would choose a little stone farmhouse in central Greece.

As soon as Nikos disappeared into the other room of the penthouse adjoining hers, she phoned the front desk and asked to be put through to Karl's room. He didn't answer his cell, so she had no choice but to leave the message that she'd arrived and to give him her room number.

Before coming upstairs, she and Nikos had stopped in several of the shops to buy her some clothes and toiletries. The good-looking saleswomen employed by the hotel had fallen all over themselves in an effort to capture Nikos's interest.

Appearing with Nikos in public meant he commanded all the attention. For once, being Tracey Loretto took a back seat. She loved it.

She loved *him* with a constant ache.

Someone had once said it was unhealthy to wish you could do your life over. Maybe it was. Still, Tracey couldn't help wondering what would have happened if she and Nikos could have spent one night alone away from her grandfather.

Except she really did know the answer to that question. Nothing would have come of it because she couldn't have left her mother.

Since it did no good to keep dwelling on the past, Tracey hurriedly showered and donned a filmy dress in a smoky-blue color Nikos had picked out. As she was slipping on her high heels, she heard a knock on the door leading into the hall.

"Tracey?" Karl called out.

"Just a moment!"

When she opened it, he rushed in and grabbed her, swinging her around.

His gaze appraised her. "You've lost weight."

"So have you."

He had the tall, wonderful looks of the dark blond German men in his ancestry, but his features were drawn. She could tell he hadn't slept well for a long time.

"Don't look now but we have company," he whispered. "If it isn't Nikos Lazaridis in the flesh. Why didn't you warn me you've been seeing him?"

"It's not what you think, but there's no time to explain now. Please don't be upset. He doesn't know why I've come to see you."

"I did knock," Nikos drawled in a voice that bordered on menacing.

Tracey whirled around. She might have known he would choose this particular moment to enter the room. At the sight of his rock-hard frame wearing a black silk shirt and gray trousers, her insides almost dissolved.

The two men took their measure of each other. On Karl's part, there was awe in the blue eyes that matched his pullover. She couldn't say the same for Nikos. Those slits of gold could well belong to a panther.

"Nikos? This is Karl Von Axel. Karl, meet Nikos Lazaridis."

"It's a pleasure." Karl extended his hand.

Nikos shook it. "When Tracey said she was meeting you, I told her I'd like the two of you to be my guests for dinner."

She caught the silent signal of pleading in Karl's eyes. He wanted to talk to her in private, but she had to appease Nikos, too.

"Before we married, Nikos offered to give us a party in New York, but time didn't permit."

"Then we'd be honored." Karl had gotten the message.

"Good. I've reserved a table for us in the restaurant. Shall we have a drink here first?"

"Fine."

"What would you like?"

"Brandy."

She watched Nikos go over to the bar and pour Karl a glass. He pulled two bottled waters from the fridge and handed the drinks around. The inscrutable expression on his carved features unsettled Tracey.

Karl took a drink, eyeing Nikos. "I see you know Tracey well enough to realize she can't tolerate alcohol."

Those golden eyes swerved to her. "Champagne was the culprit, I believe."

"That's right," Karl answered for her. "She had a glass at our wedding and became ill. It proved to be a memorable night." He swallowed the rest of his brandy.

Nikos stood there with his legs slightly apart, one hand in the pocket of his trousers while he drank his water with the other. "Tracey never told me how you two met. Was it a long courtship?"

Her pulse started to race.

"There wasn't one," Karl answered honestly.

She choked on her first sip of water.

"Why?"

Karl looked dumbfounded. "Because our marriage was arranged."

"I thought so," Nikos's voice grated.

"What else do you want to know?"

"Anything you want to tell me."

Suddenly Karl looked nervous. "I don't think I understand."

"Do you two share a child?"

"Hell no!"

"You *know* we don't." Tracey couldn't understand why Nikos was acting like this.

He cocked his dark head at Karl. "Then explain to me why you continue to contact Tracey. After all, you divorced her. I know she gives you money, but that doesn't require a phone call."

Tension filled the hotel room.

"Are you angry at me?" Karl asked her in bewilderment.

"How could she possibly be angry?" Nikos answered for her. "One phone call from you and she came running."

Nikos made a frightening adversary and had gone too far. It was up to Tracey to protect Karl.

"Let's go down to dinner, shall we?"

She put her bottle on the bar and started for the door. In two swift strides, Nikos caught up to her and put his arm around her shoulders in what could only be construed as a possessive gesture. In light of her divorce, she couldn't understand his behavior.

The three of them left the room and entered the elevator across the hall. It stopped at the floor two doors down where a white-blond man of Scandinavian descent got on. Tracey happened to look at him and was surprised to encounter a familiar frigid stare.

"Erik—"

He didn't reciprocate.

Sensing the escalating tension in the elevator, Nikos drew her closer to his hard body. He wouldn't know she was used to Erik throwing daggers at her and Karl when he saw them together.

Poor Karl. Tracey had to do something quick to end his agony. The door had just closed.

Without conscious thought, she reached in front of Nikos and pressed the stop button. It brought the elevator to a sudden halt between floors, catching the men off guard.

"Nikos? Would you keep the button pressed till I'm finished saying what needs to be said?"

With a calm she could only envy, he did her bidding.

"Erik? Since you're the reason I'm in Montreux, I couldn't be happier things have worked out this way. It saves me having to hunt you down."

Her comment caused his silver eyes to flash in total shock.

"I don't believe you've ever met Nikos Lazaridis." She turned to the man whose powerful arm had slid around her hip, sending out an even stronger signal of intimacy. She decided to take advantage of his protective instinct and use it to help Karl.

"Nikos, darling?" She glanced up at him. "This is Erik Soderhielm. He and Karl were living together before our marriage. What Erik refuses to believe is that Karl was faithful to him throughout the seven years Karl and I lived together as man and wife."

Tracey watched his eyes. She'd heard of molten gold, but she'd never seen solid gold change into a liquid state before. She knew his brilliant mind was reassessing what he thought he'd understood.

Even the all-seeing, all-knowing Helios hadn't been prepared for this revelation.

Turning to Erik, who was looking at Karl with a mixture of guilt and pain in his eyes, she said, "As soon as my grandfather died, Karl and I were able to divorce. Now that you've heard the truth from the only source who could verify it, how you choose to deal with the information is your affair.

"As you can see, Nikos is taking me to dinner. If either you or Karl would care to join us, feel free."

Before she could ask Nikos to release the

button, he'd already pressed the one for the mezzanine. Once again they were descending.

In another lightning move, Erik pushed the fourth-floor button. When the elevator stopped, he moved to the opening to prevent the doors from closing.

"I'm not hungry. Are you?" he asked Karl.

"No."

"Then let's go."

In front of everyone Karl reached for Tracey and hugged her hard. "Thank you," he whispered. "Thank you."

"I'm the one who will always be in your debt, Karl. Be happy," she whispered back.

The second the doors closed, the elevator started to go up, making her the slightest bit dizzy because it was unexpected. She jerked her head around and met Nikos's piercing gaze head-on.

"I've decided to dine alone with you."

Now that they didn't have an audience, there was nothing romantic about his declaration. No reason for pretense. His curiosity had taken a lethal turn. She shivered because she realized he wouldn't be satisfied until he'd wrung the explanation he wanted from her.

They ate in silence once room service had set up their meal on the terrace. A fairyland of twinkling lights ended at the lake's edge. Their reflection went on and on in the ever-widening ripples.

An idyllic setting of beauty and tranquility that hid the quiet storm gaining strength inside Nikos.

He'd finished his dinner and wandered over to the railing. For a long time, he looked out at the smaller yachts cruising the coastline. She sat watching him, trying to hold on to the moment.

She heard him expel his breath before he turned to her. "Did you go into your marriage knowing about him and Erik?"

"No."

"Were you looking forward to your wedding night?"

"I'd resigned myself to being a good wife to Karl."

His expression grew fierce. "You didn't answer my question."

She bit her lip. "No. I dreaded it. So did he. After I'd recovered from being sick, he told me the truth about him and Erik. I was so relieved there was truth between us, it paved the way for our friendship."

Lines marred his dark features. "Why did the marriage happen?"

"His father had made some bad financial decisions that put the monarchy in jeopardy. He was in heavy debt to my grandfather who'd invested in their country's metals.

"When he didn't get a return on his money, Grandfather devised a plan to marry me off to Karl, who was his parents' only offspring and the heir apparent. It would bring the prestige of a title, the one thing my grandfather couldn't have any other way except through marriage. In return, he would continue to subsidize Karl's father."

In one swift move, Nikos reached the table and leaned on it with his fists. "Why didn't you divorce after a decent interval?" he demanded with barely leashed civility.

Tracey started trembling. "Because I liked Karl."

"*I've* liked several women, but I never married them. You need to give me a better reason than that."

"I don't have one." She got up from the table. "Even if I did, it has no bearing on your mentoring me."

His chest rose and fell visibly, as if he were

having trouble containing the violence of his emotions.

"I'm tired, Nikos. I'm sure you are, too."

Not a word out of him.

"Thanks again for flying me here and making all the arrangements. After a good night's sleep, I'm sure we'll both feel refreshed in the morning. With my business concluded, I'm eager to get back to the farm."

On that note, she started to leave.

"Tracey—"

Pausing at the entrance to the terrace, she looked over her shoulder at him. "Yes?"

"While I was with you at the hospital, you had a nightmare that terrorized you. Whenever you want to talk about it, I'm here for you."

She would never forget it and wondered how much she'd given away in her sleep. Pasting a smile on her face, she said, "Thank you, but some things are too unspeakable to revisit. I'd like to concentrate on the future. I know you would, too.

"*Kalinihta*," she said before he could.

Nikos ushered Tracey inside his private suite in Athens. "Simon? May I present Tracey Conner."

His assistant looked up in surprise. "Nikos—I didn't know you were coming in." He got to his feet and came around his desk to shake her hand. "It's a pleasure to meet you, Ms. Conner."

Tracey smiled at him. "So you're the person who makes Nikos's life run so smoothly. I happen to know you're invaluable to him."

"Thank you," he murmured. Simon was the quiet type. Her compliments made his complexion turn a ruddy color. Tracey had a way of entrancing every man she met.

Whether in a designer dress or the jeans and leaf-green top she was wearing, her natural beauty and curves stood out.

"We're on our way back to the farm from Switzerland, Simon. I decided we'd stop in to get a file I need. If you'd call down to the restaurant and ask them to bring lunch to my office, I'd appreciate it."

"Right away."

Nikos ushered Tracey into his private office and shut the door. She wandered around, gazing out the windows at the city of Athens sprawled below them.

"I can't decide which view I like more. The

one from here or your apartment. The mansion in Buffalo is hidden in the woods. Huge as it is, I always feel enclosed and claustrophobic."

She whirled around to face Nikos. "The mere thought of remembering it makes me ill. I never want to step foot on the grounds again."

Her scars ran deep. "Understood."

"I asked Sadie to store the few things I've saved of my parents. When I go back to Buffalo to live, I'm going to buy a small, two-bedroom condo where I can see out of the windows. I need open spaces so I can breathe.

"When I've found the right place, I'll have their belongings delivered to me and incorporate them into my decor."

He studied her set features for a moment. "Have you given a lot of thought as to how you would decorate it?"

She drew in a deep breath. "I know what I don't want."

"Be more precise."

"Anything older than the year 2000 is out."

A chuckle escaped Nikos's throat. "That sounded definite enough."

"I want clean lines, lots of white with splashes

of color. No clutter. Pots of flowers. The only thing black will be my dog."

His hands tightened on the back of the chair. "Come over here and sit down, Tracey. I have something to show you."

While she did his bidding, he reached for the architect's portfolio resting against the wall and put it on the table.

"I'd like you to take a look at these and see what you think." He pulled the matching leather chair next to hers so they could view the contents together.

Inside the cover lay the top sheet with the artist's rendering of the one-story farmhouse Nikos intended to build. It showed how the old one would be incorporated into the new plans that included a swimming pool beneath the lattice overhang.

Tracey took a good five minutes studying it before she said anything. "It's lovely, Nikos," came her subdued response. Not exactly what he'd hoped for.

A knock on the door drew his attention. One of the staff wheeled in the cart with their lunch. He thanked them before removing the drawing so she could see the blueprints for each part of the house.

"If you're going to fill your home with little farmers, four spacious bedrooms like these should be plenty."

"That's the idea."

His architect had created an open design to Nikos's specifications. One alcove led to another. The kitchen was big enough for the whole family to be able to assemble and eat.

"So many large windows. You'll have that Greek sun everywhere you look, and air-conditioning to keep you comfortable. Who wouldn't be happy in such a dwelling? What will you grow on your farm besides mustard?"

"Poppies for the front of the house."

"Like the ones we flew over that first day."

He nodded. "I like their color against a white exterior."

"Well it looks like you've thought of every-thing. Thank you for letting me see your plans."

She got up and walked over to the cart to serve herself a plate of salad. Reaching for the iced tea, she said, "How soon will you be starting construction?"

"It has already begun. By the time we get back, the workmen should have cleared away the burned debris and started the dirt removal. In another day they'll be laying the foundation."

"There's going to be a lot going on out there from now on."

He hoped she was lamenting their lack of privacy. Nikos had already been dreading it.

"I've told the men they can use the farmhouse when they have to. That's why I thought it best to camp out from the beginning. During the day they can traipse back and forth without worrying about the mess they make. It's just as well you're living at the hotel."

Her enigmatic gaze shot to his. "I agree."

He'd fixed himself a plate of salad, but found he'd lost his appetite and munched on a roll instead.

"Is there any shopping you want to do in Athens before we leave?"

"No. I'd prefer to fly back to the farm. I've got a lot of work to get through today."

Ironic to think she really meant it.

"Then I'll tell the pilot we'll be up on the roof as soon as we finish eating."

"Give me a second to use the restroom and I'll join you."

After she disappeared, he drank his tea in one

go and gathered up the portfolio to take with them. He should have been relieved they were going back to the farm with the problem of Karl resolved in his mind.

Unfortunately other problems were crowding in, making chaos of his emotions. There had to be a way to break her down so she'd talk to him. Normally he wasn't a patient man, but he was going to have to develop some patience if he hoped to get the bottom of her deepest fears.

As the ground came up to meet them, Tracey got a bird's eye view of the progress already made on the farm by the construction crew. Half a dozen workmen had converged on the scene with their machinery.

Between all their equipment plus the vehicles she and Nikos owned, the place looked alive and was humming with activity.

Once the helicopter landed, Nikos helped her to climb down. When she told him she could carry her own suitcase, he ignored her and followed her inside the house with them.

One step into the dining room and she saw daylight coming from the hallway. The boards that had blocked off the bedrooms had come down. Curious to see the damage left by the fire, she walked the rest of the way inside.

At one time there'd been two small adjoining bedrooms. Now there was just one wall that had spanned both. The rest was open to the elements. Dust was flying. She could hear a machine digging.

Nikos came to stand behind her. She turned to him. "A lot of happiness went on here, didn't it?"

He nodded.

"I envy you your memories of everyone living close together, knowing your parents were right through the wall if you needed them."

"Once or twice I heard my father mutter that it was too damn close for all of us," he declared.

"But when you look back, would you have had it any other way?"

He rubbed his lower lip absently. "Probably not."

She looked at the scorched wall and saw a number of holes where pictures had once hung. She also noticed some lines and numbers going up the wall at the side of the doorjamb. They'd been made with a pencil.

"What are these?"

His eyes smiled, a rare occurrence for him.

"Papa used to measure me and Leon every year to see how much we'd grown."

Tracey looked up to see the highest mark. "It that one yours? I can't read the writing."

"No. Leon's. His eighteenth birthday. I was sixteen at the time. Here's my mark." He pointed to it. "I didn't catch up to him for another year."

"You have to save this!" she cried. "It's a precious piece of family history."

He eyed her strangely.

"I'd give anything to have such a memory," she explained. "Ask one of the men to cut out that strip of wallboard and save it. You can find a place to put it somewhere else for your children to see. Maybe in the laundry room I saw in the blueprints.

"Think how fun for them to start measuring themselves against their father and uncle. If I were your child, I'd be delighted."

A stunned look crept over his striking face. "You have me stymied, Tracey. In one breath you call me Helios, in the next you imagine I'm your brother. Now you're talking about being my child."

Embarrassed, she said, "Don't mind me. I

talk too much, and am probably getting on your nerves."

"You need to talk."

She started back down the hall to the dining room. "Thanks for the psychological evaluation, Doctor," she called over her shoulder. "How about putting on your farmer's hat and explaining the best way to get rid of flea beetles?"

He turned on the fan and adjusted it so it would blow on her. "If you discover the presence of a few, it isn't cause for serious concern."

Tracey sat down at the table and opened her ledger. "But what if there *is* an infestation? I want to be prepared. It won't hurt to plan a budget that includes the chemicals to get rid of them."

"I'm impressed you're so on top of things. If you should find them numerous and feeding damage is present, then you'll want to control them with a good chemical."

She found the spot in the chapter that addressed eradication. "Which one do you think is better? Malathion, or carbyrl?"

"Malathion always worked for Papa."

"Thank you. I'll call the co-op and get a price on it." She made the notation without looking at him.

"If you have any other questions, I'll be back in a few minutes. I need to talk to the foreman."

"Go ahead. I've got a ton of reading to do."

He stood next to her chair as if he were a stranger in his own home.

Please leave, Nikos.

The second he walked out the front door, relief swept over her. Since he'd shown her the portfolio, she'd been in so much pain she didn't know how she was going to make it through the next hour, let alone the next few months.

Another woman would be living with him here one day soon. The less Tracey thought about it— the less he discussed it with her—the better.

How could he know his house plans spoke to her heart? It was exactly the kind of home she pictured for herself. Stark-white inside and out with Greek archways typical of the kind you saw in the villas on Mykonos or Corfu.

Out of respect for Nikos, she'd never come to his country where the media would mock her and smear her name and pictures right in his face. But she'd seen pictures of cubicle villages dotting the Greek Islands in the Aegean she'd love to visit.

He'd be creating a taste of them right here on his own piece of earth he'd inherited over several generations. His children would play here. They'd be wanted and loved. The woman who loved him would have the right to get up with him every morning, go to bed with him every night. And thrill to every second of her life with him in between.

"Ms. Conner?"

Startled out of her reverie, she looked up from the book she hadn't been able to concentrate on and saw that one of the workmen had come in from the hallway. "Yes?"

"*Kyrie* Lazaridis said you should show me what you want done with the wall out there."

Tracey reeled, unable to believe Nikos was letting her make that decision. On some level he must have liked the idea. She was absurdly happy about it, and slid out of the chair.

When she showed him the spot, she measured six inches from the doorjamb. "Can you cut the wallboard in a straight line from the ceiling to the floor and leave this whole piece intact?"

He scratched his head. "I will try."

"Thank you. It's very important all these pencil marks remain untouched or smeared. Try to keep it as clean as possible."

"I'll take great care."

"Are you going to do it now?"

"Yes."

"Then I'll stay and help you."

In the distance she could see Nikos walking around with the head contractor. They were deep in discussion. She remained in the doorway and waited for the short, wiry man to come back with his power saw.

He measured and drew a line, then began cutting with expertise. It was a lot trickier proposition when he had to make the same cut next to the doorjamb.

Tracey stood on the other side and pressed on the wallboard as he progressed. When he'd finished, the strip was loose except for a few places where it had been nailed to the two-by-four.

"In order to get the nails out, it's going to make small holes."

"That's all right. They're not by the writing."

With painstaking care, he removed them and suddenly the strip was freestanding.

"I'll help you carry it down the hall. Where do you want to keep it?"

"Right here on the floor in front of the living-room window, face up." They gently laid it down.

She beamed at him. "Thank you so much."

His raisin colored eyes twinkled. "You're welcome."

When he'd gone, she reached for her purse and hurried outside to the car. She needed to run into town and get a transparent sealer and brush.

Nikos was too far away for her to bother him with her plans. He could always call her on her cell if he needed to get hold of her.

On her way, she phoned Maria to find out the address of a good paint store. The other woman suggested she drive up in front of the hotel and Ari would show her. It would be easier.

A few minutes later she saw Ari waving her down. As she slowed, he jumped in the car and flashed her a white smile. "Bless you, Tracey. You've saved me from having to help clear up a minor disaster in the kitchen between the chefs. They're too temperamental to be working together."

She chuckled.

"I'm yours for the rest of the afternoon. Mama says you need paint."

"That and a newspaper."

"I know where to get both. Keep going down the street and turn right at the next corner."

When she parked near the store in question, she explained exactly what she wanted. "Make sure it's the kind that won't dissolve pencil writing. I only need a little bit and a medium-sized brush. Here's my credit card."

He didn't take it. "I'll put it on Papa's account." Before she could argue with him, he'd gone and was back in a flash with his purchase and a newspaper tucked under his arm.

Once they were on their way to the farm, he said, "I thought you were supposed to be working on your crop."

"I am, but a little project came up I needed to do."

"What is it?"

"I'll show you when we get there."

"This sounds mysterious."

She darted him a teasing smile. "I think you'll find it more interesting than anyone else."

"Now I'm really curious." He gazed at her profile. "This is a nice little car."

"I think it is, too."

"You could have bought any kind you wanted."

"This is exactly what I wanted, Ari. What on earth would I do with a Ferrari?"

"Drive me around so I could have fun in it."

Ari was hilarious.

"Do you have a car?"

"Not yet. As soon as I turn eighteen I'm moving out and getting me one."

"Where are you going?"

"To college in Athens."

"That's wonderful. What will you study?"

"Resort management. One day I plan to own a string of them."

"With vision like that, I have no doubt you'll be successful."

"Thanks. Will you come and see me after I'm settled in an apartment?"

"Of course. I'll bring you a housewarming present."

"Just you will be enough."

She grinned at him. "You know something, Ari? You're full of it."

"And you're gorgeous."

Tracey decided the best way to handle him was not to respond to a comment like that.

Nikos was still talking with the foreman as she pulled up the track and turned off the car. The two of them got out. She hurried inside the farm-house ahead of Ari.

"How can I help?"

"Will you spread enough newspapers so I can paint this strip of wallboard on them?"

"Sure."

He really was a terrific help.

"Okay. Now I'll lay it out carefully."

Ari hunkered down to help her. "Why are you doing this?"

When she explained what it was, his whole face ignited. "That's Papa's mark at the top?" he blurted incredulously.

"Yes, at the same age you are now, give or take a few months."

"And that's Uncle Nikos's below his?"

"When he was sixteen."

"I bet I'm taller than Papa. Let's find out."

"First you need to take off your shoes. I believe they did this in their stocking feet."

Off came his shoes, then he lay down along side it.

She studied his length against the board. "You're going to have to scrunch higher so your heels are even with the end of the board."

He moved a little bit. "Is this better?"

"Maybe another half inch."

The adjustment worked. "Perfect. Now don't move. I need to get a pen out of my purse."

As soon as that was accomplished, she got down on her hands and knees with the top of his head facing her. "I'll make a mark on the newspaper, and we'll see who reigns king in the Lazaridis family.

"Grr. This pen— Just a minute, Ari." She pressed the point against the newspaper to make it write. "Okay. Now. Hold still."

She bent over and cupped his chin to steady him while she drew a line past his head.

"What's going on here?"

Her head flew back, startled by the peremptory tone in Nikos's voice.

Ari smiled up at his uncle without moving. "I slipped and got the wind knocked out of me. She was just giving me mouth-to-mouth resuscitation."

Judging by the hardness of Nikos's jaw, it was the wrong thing to say to him. This was one time Ari had gone too far.

Tracey stood up. "I was measuring him to see if he was taller than his father."

"What's the verdict?" Ari asked, scrambling to his feet in a nimble move.

"See for yourself." She avoided Nikos's narrowed gaze.

Ari looked at the mark she'd made. "Hmm. That couldn't be right. According to this I'm a half inch shorter than Papa."

"It could be wrong, Ari. After it's part of the new wall, then you can try it again to be certain."

"Great. Don't tell Papa anything yet, Uncle Nikos."

"I wouldn't dream of it." His voice sounded cavernous.

"Shall I paint it for you now, Tracey?"

"That's very accommodating of you, Ari," Nikos interjected before she could, but he didn't sound quite as savage as before. "Let me help you carry it out to the back porch, then I won't be bothered by the fumes when I sleep tonight."

"Sure."

Tracey followed them through the house, holding the sack and newspapers. She laid the papers down in front of the washer and dryer so Ari could get started.

While they were busy, she went back to the dining room to finish the rest of the chapter. After reading the same paragraph five times, she realized she was through studying for the day.

Too restless to sit, she walked outside through the front door to see the progress the workmen had been making. Only two men were left and it looked as if they were getting ready to go home for the day.

Nikos had said he'd been making plans to retire for the last year. She no longer wondered why he hadn't found another farm for her to work. By building his house and mentoring her at the same time, he was killing the proverbial two birds with one stone.

Her gaze wandered to the far distance where she could see the Meteora. Maybe when she drove back to town and dropped Ari off, she'd take the road that led to the monastery on top and play tourist. The key to not thinking too much was to stay busy.

"Ari?" she called to him when she entered the house. "I'm ready to go home when you are."

"Coming."

Not wanting to face Nikos, she picked up her suitcase and carried it to her car, putting it on the back seat. In another minute Ari jogged up to the car and got in, bringing the smell of fumes with him. A somber Nikos, looking more handsome than she'd ever seen him, stood in the doorway with his shirtsleeves rolled up.

The sight of his powerful shoulders and tall, rock-hard body leveraged against the doorjamb of his family home would stay with her forever. She wished she had a camera to preserve this moment so she could feast her eyes on him when she went to bed.

She waved to him before backing out to the road.

Once on their way, Ari's cell phone rang. He spoke in rapid Greek, then turned to her. "Mama says Dimitri Chrystos has left you a message."

Oh no. "Is that the only reason she called?"

"No. She needs me in the kitchen. Are you going to go out with him?"

It was none of his business, but she couldn't say that to him.

"No."

"Will you let me take you dancing tonight after work?"

"No."

"Did Uncle Nikos tell you not to go out with me?"

She gripped the steering wheel tighter. "Ari— I'm a recently divorced woman enjoying my freedom from any pressure."

"I hear you. So what you're saying is, you need a little more time."

"Yes."

"Okay. I can live with that."

She was glad to hear it since she wanted to remain friends with him and not hurt his pride.

To prevent further conversation, she turned on the radio until she found a station playing Greek rock. That seemed to please him.

"You're not coming in?" he asked when she let him off in front.

"Not yet."

She watched him start to say something, then refrain.

"Thank you for buying those materials and helping me."

"It was fun." He broke into a broad grin. "I really had Uncle Nikos going there for a minute."

Tracey rolled her eyes. "Do you do that kind of thing often?"

He cocked his head. "Only when I can tell he's uptight about something. He doesn't like me hanging around you."

"I think it's more a case of his wanting you to enjoy young women of your own age."

"No. He was really upset."

Worried about where this conversation was headed, she said, "Can you keep a secret?"

"Sure."

"I mean you can't tell anyone, Ari. This is just between you and me."

"I swear."

"He thinks it's his fault I got heatstroke, so he's being overprotective. If he seems tense it's also because he knows I've been fragile since the divorce. He's trying to help me get tough enough to face a boardroom of powerful men who eat women in business for breakfast.

"Nikos is the kind of man who takes wounded birds like me under his wing. He's a hero because he can't help it. Couple that with the fact that he loves you very much and wants you to make good choices, and his burden grows heavy at times. Do you understand what I'm saying?"

He studied her for a moment, then leaned over and kissed her cheek. "I do. See you later."

She said goodbye and joined the mainstream of traffic. On the outskirts of town she saw the sign for the monasteries and followed the route past the village of Kastraki into the hills.

Tracey wished Nikos were with her and felt a stab in her heart as she kept winding toward the awesome pinnacles. Her progress was slowed by the number of tourists going up and down.

The sunset gave off a pink glow, glazing the giant rocks in an overlay that seemed out of this world. At the approach to the St. Nicholas Anapafsas monastery, she pulled into a parking area.

There was a sign indicating that women entering the edifice needed to wear sleeved dresses. No pants or shorts allowed. That ruled out her visit for tonight, but it was all right. She could get out and view the vista from this vantage point. The rocky promontories and wooden bridges crossing dizzying chasms fascinated her.

As she reached for the handle, the car door opened.

A small cry escaped her throat when she saw Nikos standing there. Her thoughts seemed to have conjured him up. "Have you been following me?" she said so he wouldn't guess her true feelings. She needed to catch her breath before she could find the strength to move.

His eyes wandered over her face. "Isn't it obvious?"

"Yes. I just don't understand why."

He leaned against the opening, barring her exit. "Ari seemed all too happy to go off with you. Before you think I'm about to blame you, let me finish. I can see all the running is on his part. But his father is concerned, so I decided it might be wise to intervene if I had to."

She smoothed the hair off her forehead. "I had a little talk with him on the way back to town. I think he understands now."

His dark head came closer, making it difficult for her to breathe. "Understands what?"

"I told him I've been in a bad place since the divorce and need my space."

"He's still young enough to see that as a challenge."

Her eyes flashed. "Would you have had me hurt him by saying I don't date little boys with no money? Or should I have said I'm out for all I can get from his uncle, so run along home to Mama."

Shadows formed on his face, which looked chiseled in the fading light.

"You know what I think, Nikos? Though you meant well by bringing me to the farm, everything's getting a little too complicated. I'm not saying I'm going to quit, but I am going to do all of us a favor by moving to another hotel. I passed one in Kastraki that will be perfect."

The idea hadn't come to her until she was saying it.

"If you do that, you'll insult my family," he ground out.

"Then what's the answer?"

"He'll be leaving for college in a month."

"I know. Until then, I'll try to avoid him."

A strange sound came out of him. He stood up. "It's too dark to see anything tonight. You shouldn't be up here alone. I'll follow you back to the hotel."

"All right."

"Tracey—"

"What?" Her pulse was throbbing.

"Your interest in preserving that strip of wall-board meant a lot to me."

In the next breath he leaned inside and brushed his mouth against hers. He'd meant it as a thank-you kiss, but he shouldn't have done it. Fire spread to every atom of her sensitized body.

If he ever did that again, she wouldn't be able to hold back her response.

In three weeks' time Tracey couldn't believe the progress that had been made. After all the soil preparation, Elias had come with the seed planter. That was when the fun had begun.

All those thousands and thousands of tiny seeds she'd bought at the co-op were now tucked in their shallow bed of soil. She'd worked with Nikos to place the bands of fertilizer below and along the sides of the seed furrows. Now she couldn't wait for them to sprout.

Each morning she'd put on the hat Ari had bought her and walked around her acre of ground, surveying every aspect. Waterlogged soil would destroy a new crop so she had to keep a tight control on the irrigation.

Though there'd been more observing than hands-on moments, she felt a sense of accomplishment totally foreign to her.

The heat didn't bother her nearly as much. She could stay at the farm all day and felt fine. Nikos had given her a key to the house. Once the manual labor was done, she'd go inside.

Over lunch she'd read everything she could about weed-and disease-control from books Nikos had supplied. The rest of the time she worked on the accounts and studied problems he'd given her to solve connected with information from the company's quarterly statements. Many were the evenings she didn't go back to the hotel until dinner.

If she hadn't suffered heat exhaustion, she would never have ended up living there. Going to the hospital had changed everything. Nikos hadn't asked her to come back to the farmhouse. She missed the nights with him. Nothing would ever be the same again. How could it when he was making plans for his future that didn't include her?

Ari managed to be around every time she walked through reception. She was getting used to him begging her to take a night off and go out with him, but she always turned him down.

Not just because she'd made that promise to Nikos. Ari was at the age where he wanted to be in love. Let it be a special girl he could marry one day, the kind Nikos wanted for himself.

Tracey's life was uncomplicated right now. When she fell into bed after her dinner, she went straight to sleep, plum tired in a wonderful way because she'd put in an honorable day's work.

Now when she looked in the mirror, she hardly recognized herself with her farmer's tan. But she needed to do something about her hair. The roots were showing a brighter red than the rest of it.

Since their return from Montreux, Nikos had refrained from talking about her past. Most of the time they discussed farming or worked in companionable silence. No more scathing remarks, or slings and arrows to dodge. No more questions she couldn't bring herself to answer.

Sometimes he left for the whole day and she was

on her own. Several times he hadn't come back by the time she left to drive into town. Only once had he joined everyone at the hotel for dinner.

He still had loose ends of business to attend to in Athens. She suspected he flew there to enjoy a night of pleasure at his condo.

Though Tracey might not have his nights, for the most part she had his days, which she cherished in the deepest recess of her being. To work with him on this farm was the closest she had ever come to pure happiness.

And she had a memory she would always hug to herself of the two of them entwined in his kitchen, kissing each other with unbridled hunger.

It had to be enough.

"Tracey?" a voice called to her as she walked into the hotel foyer. For once it wasn't Ari's.

"Good evening, Maria. How are you?"

Nikos's sister-in-law raised her expressive eyebrows. "I'll be fine when you've talked to Dimitri Chrystos."

The situation was growing out of control. "You know his family?"

"Yes. They're good people. Since he met you, he's been a very persistent man who has phoned the hotel at least six times this week. I've left the messages in your box."

She handed Tracey the most recent one.

"I know. I'm sorry, Maria. I've come home so tired every night, I've been putting other things off. Today I spent the whole time indoors studying about pests and sprays."

"Better you than me," Maria quipped with a chuckle.

"I promise to call him the minute I go upstairs."

"Thank you," she said with her hand over her heart. The gesture caused both of them to burst into laughter. Tracey loved Maria's happy nature and wanted to emulate it.

"See you later."

She used the stairs to reach her room. Once inside she went straight to the phone at the side of her bed to return Dimitri's call. She caught him as he was leaving work.

His voice brightened when he discovered who it was, and he immediately asked her out for the evening. Being as diplomatic as possible, she told him she was seeing someone else, but was flattered he'd thought of her.

After thanking him, she hung up the phone

and headed for the shower. Maybe she'd get dressed up and go to a local restaurant for dinner. Tonight she was feeling more restless than usual.

Nikos pulled the truck up in front of the hotel. He'd been in Athens most of the day. After the helicopter had dropped him off at the farm, he'd seen something that had prompted him to drive into town for Tracey.

"She's not here," Ari blurted the second Nikos walked through the doors.

Nikos's good mood vanished in an instant.

His nephew's unwelcome news, delivered with a bitter edge uncharacteristic of Ari, wasn't exactly the reception Nikos had been expecting.

"Why the scowl?"

"I can't compete with a guy who drives his father's Lexus when he wants to impress a woman."

The only man who owned a Lexus in Kalambaka was Stavros Chrystos. His son Dimitri worked for him and had undoubtedly sold Tracey her car. End of mystery.

"You saw her leave with him?"

"No, but I'm sure she went to meet him somewhere."

Not necessarily.

"The right woman is impressed with a man's integrity, not the size of his bank balance."

"That's rich coming from you—" Ari was in a nasty temper.

One dark brow dipped. Nikos took him aside where no one could hear them. "Why do you think I'm still single? I wasn't as lucky as your father. Did you know I had a crush on your mother when I was your age?"

Ari's expression sobered.

"But the only person she ever saw was Leon. When we both left the farm, he begged me to come to work at the hotel with him. But I was too jealous of his relationship with your mother, so I took off for Athens."

Ari's gaze studied Nikos for a long time. "Papa thinks you don't like him."

"I've always worshipped my older brother. He knew what he wanted and didn't hesitate to go after it."

"But that's what he says about you!"

Nikos shook his head. "I always wanted to be

a farmer, but it took until this last year for me to admit it." It had taken a certain mermaid to swim up to him and ask if she could pick his brains for him to do something about it.

"Papa doesn't know how you feel."

"It's time I told him."

He patted Ari's shoulder, then walked down the hall to Leon's office. He found his brother going over the accounts, and shut the door.

Leon looked up in surprise. "How come you're here this late?"

"Try twenty-one years too late."

His brother stared at him in puzzlement. "What do you mean?"

"I just came from talking with Ari. He says you're under the misconception that I don't love my elder brother. Nothing could be further from the truth. I'm here to set the record straight."

An hour later, he left Leon's office feeling better than he'd felt in years. The bear hug they'd given each other punctuated the end to the hurtful misunderstandings of the past.

But eradicating the baggage he'd been carrying unnecessarily all these years seemed to exacer-

bate another pain that had been growing and fes-
tering like a malignant tumor.

Nikos left the hotel and got back in the truck.
It was 10:30 p.m. Tracey ought to be back soon.
Eleven o'clock rolled around. At eleven-ten he
saw Tracey walking alone toward the hotel.
Nikos sucked in with his scorched lungs.

He got out of the truck and reached the hotel
doors ahead of her. She let out a little cry of
surprise when she saw him.

"Nikos—"

Her breathing sounded shallow. In the frothy
blue dress she'd bought in Montreux outlining
her rich curves, her beauty took *his* breath.

"Ari said you were out with Dimitri Chrystos."

"Your nephew assumed wrong."

Relieved by the news, he said, "I'm glad you're
still up so I didn't have to waken you. Something's
happened at the farm you need to see."

An anxious look entered her eyes. "Has there
been flooding from the irrigation?"

"That's for you to find out. You're the farmer."

She bit the soft underside of her lip. "I'll
change and be right down."

True to her word, she was back within five

minutes wearing a yellow top with jeans and her sensible boots. He helped her into the truck and they headed for the farm.

He gave her enchanting profile a cursory glance. "Did you eat dinner out?"

"Yes, at the same taverna where we had breakfast. I enjoyed the bouzouki music."

"You probably gave every man in sight a heart attack."

She rolled her eyes. "If I did, I wasn't aware of it. Now please don't keep me in suspense. Won't you give me a hint what's wrong? I've tried to do every step right."

"Have I faulted you for anything?"

She shook her head. "I'm just nervous."

"We're almost there."

A minute later he drove up the track. Before he had time to shut off the motor, she jumped down from the cab and started running around the side of the farmhouse.

He followed after her at a slower pace, allowing her to make the discovery for herself. It wasn't long in coming.

"Nikos—" she cried in despair, standing next

to one of the furrows. "My crop has been infested with tiny little *worms!* There are *thousands* of them. I can't believe it!"

CHAPTER NINE

NIKOS PASSED A HAND over his mouth, fighting the desire to laugh.

She lifted her tormented face to him in the moonlight. He saw the trail of her tears against her tanned cheeks. "The books talked about flea beetles and caterpillars, but nothing was said about worms!"

"Are you sure that's what they are?"

"I don't know what else they could be."

He watched her get down on her knees and bend over to inspect them.

"They're not wiggling." She reached out to touch one. A gasp followed. "These aren't worms…."

Nikos moved closer. "Then what are they?"

"They're my little seedlings." He heard the awe in her voice. "They've emerged!"

She jumped up, turning a glowing face to him. "My crop—it's coming up!"

"How could you have ever doubted it?"

In the next breath, she closed the distance between them and threw her arms around him, laughing and crying at the same time. "I'm a farmer!" She threw her head back. "This is the most exciting moment of my life! Thank you dear Nikos."

She raised up on tiptoe and kissed both his cheeks, European-style. The touch of her lips was like the sun's caress, warming him in the areas of his soul that had never known its warmth before.

"Maybe now you understand why a farmer doesn't work at night."

She pulled away from him, blushing to the roots of her glorious red hair. "I can't believe I ever asked you that question. Promise me you'll never tell anybody."

"If I promise, then you have to do something for me."

"Anything," she came back in such a serious tone, it shook him.

"Stay here tonight. I feel like celebrating my only student's success and would rather not have to drive you back to the hotel."

She looked without striving into his eyes. "I don't want to go back."

"Good."

"When I wake up tomorrow, I'm going to run outside and see if the seedlings are any bigger."

Nikos smiled.

"I know you're laughing, but haven't you ever wanted to watch something grow? I mean, when did those little shoots suddenly pop up from the soil? I didn't see them there yesterday. Yet tonight the whole acre is polka-dotted with them."

"I'm not laughing at you, Tracey. You remind me of myself when I was young, trying to catch something growing. I never did. You'd have to film it with a special camera and see the changes frame by frame."

"It wouldn't be the same."

"You're right."

Reaching for her hand, they walked toward the farmhouse. It was then he experienced a feeling of déjà vu.

When he remembered his dreams, they were always of him walking hand in hand with this woman through a field. Words weren't necessary because their minds and bodies were so attuned. Complete.

Once he and Tracey entered the house, he got out the bottles of cold water and fresh plums to celebrate. After he'd turned off the lights, they both got ready for bed. He lent her one of his oversize T-shirts. She'd offered to sleep on the broken cot lying on the floor.

Nikos shook his head. "I like it down here. Now I can move around all I want without fear of another earthquake."

Gentle laughter poured out of Tracey as they both remembered the moment that had brought an abrupt end to his rapture.

She lay stomach down on her cot, her head resting on her arms while she stared at him.

Their eyes met. "What are you thinking about so intently?" he asked.

"Sprawled beneath that sheet, you look like a picture I've seen of Helios warming himself on a flowered hillside of the Peloponnese."

He frowned. "Tracey—do you ever see me as a man?"

She dangled her arm over the edge of the cot. "To be honest, the two of you are indistinguishable. That comes from my having a fanciful nature. While other girls dreamed of comic-book heroes, I got lost in the lore of the Olympians."

He rolled on his side to face her. "If my grandfather had the habit of locking me in a room, I'm sure I would have created a mythical world, too. What else did he do to you?"

The silence lasted too long before she said, "I've already told you."

"Not everything."

She buried her face in the pillow. "Some things are too evil to talk about."

Her words raised the hairs on the back of his neck. "You need to tell someone or you'll become ill. Why not me? You trusted me enough to seek my help in the first place. I want to understand what power he had to force you to marry a man you didn't love."

She stirred and lifted her head. "He had a lot of power, Nikos."

"Every time I came to the mansion, I felt like I was walking into an armed fortress."

"That's what it was…." Her words came out on a strangled breath, horrifying Nikos, who'd already figured it out.

"From my first recollections of life we were all Grandfather's prisoners. After Daddy died, I wasn't allowed to go anywhere or do anything without one of the guards with me.

"Grandfather explained that because he had so much money, Mother and I were a target for kidnappers. He was simply keeping us safe. We didn't believe him and clung to each other for survival. I was never left alone."

Nikos felt as if a lightning bolt had passed through his body. "I can vouch for that."

"Mother and I agreed he was a sadist. He liked torturing me by letting me get a peek at you once in a while. I'm convinced that's why he brought you to the mansion at all.

"He mapped out my life. All through private school, he had someone watching me. He ordered guards to watch me coming and going. I don't have proof, but I think he arranged the car accident that killed my father. He hated Daddy."

Nikos raised up. "Why?"

"Because Grandfather had hired him to be a guard at the mansion, and Daddy betrayed that trust by falling in love with Mother and marrying her in secret. They were planning to run away, but Grandfather found out and brought them back.

"He was a sick man who beat Mother when she was younger. That's the reason she was so terrified of him."

"Dear God—she told you this?"

"No," Tracey whispered. "When Grandfather came to my bedroom on the night I told him I wouldn't marry a man I'd never met, he warned me that if I didn't, he'd do the same to me as he did to Mother. It was only what we deserved."

White-hot with fury, Nikos leaped to his feet and reached blindly for her. "Did he beat you, Tracey?"

She didn't answer him. Shudder after shudder was shaking her body.

"Tell me," he urged, rocking her in his arms while she broke down sobbing.

"He was built like a bull. So strong. He hit me so hard, I was knocked unconscious. When I came to, my arm and head were so swollen, Mother insisted the doctor come. He said I had a broken arm and set it. I had to pretend I'd fallen down the stairs."

"Mother begged me to marry Karl. She felt it might be my only means of escape from the horror she'd lived with all her life."

Nikos kissed her hair, her cheeks. The salt from her tears was like an astringent elixir, bonding them in her grief. That grief had become his.

Devastated by what he'd heard, he carried her over to his bed and put her down. Then he lay next to her on the cot built for one and drew her into his arms, covering them with the sheet.

She burrowed her face between his neck and shoulder. For a time, her gut-wrenching sobs resounded in the room. Slowly they subsided into heart breaking whimpers.

Like a child who gave herself up to a parent in total trust, this poor little rich girl who'd never known a moment's safety in the whole of her life allowed Nikos to gentle her.

After the unconscionable way he'd treated her, the privilege brought him to tears.

"*Agape mou*," he murmured the endearment over and over until well into the night.

Toward morning he felt her stir. "Nikos?"

"I'm right here. Are you having another bad dream?"

"If you mean like that nightmare in the hospital, no."

"It was your grandfather who terrified you."

"Yes."

"At first I thought it had to be Karl."

"No. Karl lived in terror of his father doing something terrible to Erik. They had to be secretive. That's why I partied openly with other men so the press would exploit it. His father believed I was unfaithful. It kept him from blaming Karl over our failed marriage."

The hideous revelations came flying at Nikos so hard and fast he was stunned by them.

"Grandfather's sudden fatal heart attack was the miracle mother and I had been praying for so I could get out of my marriage. To release us both. But we still had to be careful that it looked like I had betrayed my husband. I didn't want his father to find out about Erik."

"You did a good job, Tracey. You had me believing your fiction," Nikos muttered in self-abnegation.

"I had to do it to protect him. He's lived in his own sort of prison for years. We needed each other to survive. But with that hurdle over, I had to start thinking how I was going to survive at Loretto's. That's when I found myself gravitating to you.

"In that nightmare, I—I'd been dreaming about you. But it was all distorted. We were on the yacht and I'd asked you to marry me because I needed you to hide me from my grandfather."

Nikos groaned.

"You told me you would agree, but in exchange I had to work on your farm. I told you I'd do anything, so you arranged our ceremony below deck with Giorgios and Stella.

"When the time came, you gave me a beautiful diamond, and I gave you a yellow sapphire I'd bought in New York to match your eyes. After we'd said our vows, you got me to admit I loved you. I asked if you were angry about that because I hadn't told you before.

"You gave me this strange smile and said I was the one who was going to be angry because you didn't love me. You couldn't love a woman like Tracey Loretto, and you were sending me to work the farm by myself because you were in love with someone else."

He cringed when he thought of his own cruelty to her. Nikos didn't feel worthy of the tiniest red-gold hair on her beautiful head.

"I told you I was afraid I wouldn't be able to do the work alone, and you said it was either that or you would send me back to my grandfather. But I knew I couldn't go back. I'd rather die—"

Finally Nikos had his explanation!

Only God knew how many nights she'd been plagued by nightmares where she was trying to get away from that monster.

"It was a terrible dream, nothing more." He smoothed the hair off her forehead.

"Dreams reveal the truth, Nikos. No man could love me."

He pressed his cheek against her hair. "I love you."

"That's because you're so good, Nikos. Tonight you've been my father confessor. But we both know I'm a failure in life. I don't know how you can bear to comfort me."

Her words almost destroyed him.

"Hush, Tracey. You're still dreaming. Go back to sleep. I won't let anything hurt you."

"I know you won't. You're Helios."

No dammit. I'm a man who may have lost the prize because I wasn't the all-seeing until it was too late.

* * *

Since the night Tracey had revealed her darkest secrets to Nikos, he hadn't changed. Despite his knowing the truth, he was still her mentor.

But there'd been a change inside her. It was like being freed from prison. She no longer felt threatened by other people's judgments of her. Nikos's opinion was the only thing that mattered.

The men at the board meeting could do their worst. She was ready for them as she stood outside the farmhouse with her suitcase, waiting for the helicopter to come and get her.

She looked all around her, delighted to see her acre covered in healthy plants. Nikos had told her that in another week, buds would appear and everything would be in full flower. After that would come the harvest, and the sale of her crop. Her gift to him.

Whether she ended up in the black or the red, she didn't know. But the experiment had turned into a lesson of life she wouldn't have missed for the world.

It was going to be harvest time for Nikos, too. Soon he would be living here and getting married. The builders had framed the new farmhouse and were already starting to put on the roof. The entire farm had been transformed. She would never have guessed it could look like this when the helicopter had first set her down in a desolate field of stubble.

In the quiet of the evening came the whirring sound of the rotor blades. The helicopter would be landing any minute now. She could fly to Athens knowing she'd taken care of everything and was leaving prepared.

The Loretto company jet was standing by to take her to New York City. It would be her one and only flight in it. After she'd spent a day there taking care of business, she would fly to Buffalo in the Loretto helicopter. Landing on top of the Loretto building in time for the board meeting would make a statement the men would never forget.

"Are you sure you don't want me to fly as far as Athens with you?"

She turned to Nikos, who looked sinfully handsome in thigh-molding jeans and a sport shirt whose sleeves banded biceps most men would kill for. Since they'd come here six weeks ago, his black hair had grown longer and curlier. She'd heard him say he needed a haircut, but she was glad he hadn't gotten around to it yet.

In the fading light, this was the picture of him she wanted to remember—his golden eyes intent on her face and figure—his arresting features more pronounced because he was her champion and was worried about her first boardroom experience.

"I'm positive," she answered him.

The helicopter set down where the road met the track.

Nikos picked up her suitcase, then flashed her a surprised glance. "This is heavy."

"I'm taking my books to read on the plane."

He clasped her arm to walk her the rest of the way before he set her luggage inside. Turning to her, he said, "I don't like the idea of letting you go alone."

She smiled up at him. "Nikos. You're so used to taking care of me, you don't know when to let go. How am I going to convince those men I'm a power to contend with if you're there holding my hand?"

His mouth thinned to a tight line. "When will you be back?"

"I'm not sure. Three days, maybe four at the most."

"I want a time," he bit out.

"I'll phone you." She raised up on tiptoe to kiss his cheek. "Wish me luck."

"You don't need it," he muttered. "You're ready."

"Thanks to you." She blew him a kiss.

Watching her fly away and disappear into the night was like being flung into a black void where there was no up or down, no point of reference. All he felt was a soul-shattering disorientation too profound to put into words.

His arm could still feel the unnatural weight of her suitcase. He frowned before walking swiftly to her car.

It was locked up. The only thing inside was her straw hat that lay on the front passenger seat like always, yet a growing sense of alarm had him chasing back inside the farmhouse.

He walked around, looking for anything out of the ordinary. The dining-room table had been cleared of her ledger and farming books. She'd taken the reports, too, leaving no signs that she'd ever been here. Naturally there wouldn't be any. Not when she'd lived at the hotel.

Nikos rubbed the back of his neck.

Why was he feeling a sense of loss this acute? Was it because they'd never been separated before?

That couldn't be the reason. There'd been times in the last six weeks when he'd flown to Athens alone in order to facilitate retirement issues. Some days they'd barely seen each other in passing.

So why was this different?

You know the answer to that, Lazaridis. Because tonight she'd been the one to leave you.

He reached in the fridge and drained a can of beer, hoping it would take the edge off his nerves. It didn't.

She was gone, and she didn't know when she'd be back. He hadn't liked her response a little while ago, and he liked it less now.

Functioning on gut instinct, he grabbed his wallet and keys, and took off for town in the truck. As he barreled along the road, he had no cognizance of his surroundings. By the time he reached the hotel and parked, he realized she was probably aboard the Loretto jet by now, ready to take off.

He strode through the hotel doors and headed

straight for Ari, who was manning the front desk
with another employee.

His nephew saw him coming. "What's wrong,
Uncle Nikos? You look sick."

"I'm all right. I need the key card to Tracey's
room. She left something she needs. I told her I'd
pick it up when I came into town."

"Sure." Ari went over to her box and handed
it to him.

Nikos grabbed it and raced up the stairs three
at a time. Finding her room, he ran the card over
the strip and opened the door.

At first glance his heart failed him.

He dashed over to the house phone and rang
reception. His nephew answered.

"Why didn't you tell me Tracey had checked
out, Ari?"

"If she did, I'm not surprised."

Ari's comment caused his temper to flare.
"Would you care to explain that remark?"

"Wait there and I'll be right up, but you have
to promise not to bite my head off."

Too full of adrenaline, he slammed the phone
on the hook, ready to explode. But Ari wasn't the
reason for his meltdown.

Forcing himself to get some control, he walked over to the door and opened it for his nephew, who hurried down the hall toward him.

Ari glanced around the room. "She really is gone, huh?"

Nikos took a calming breath. "What do you know about it?"

His nephew eyed him frankly. "How come you let her go when you're in love with her? Don't act like isn't true. I knew it the minute you introduced me to her. The whole family knew it. Tracey's the only one who's in the dark."

"Because I've been a damn fool."

"For once I agree. Listen, Uncle Nikos, she's so in love with you it's sickening. She said you're the stuff heroes are made of. You should have heard her go on and on.

"If a woman like Tracey ever loved me a tenth as much as she loves you, I'd kiss the ground forever."

"That shows the difference in our ages, Ari. When I catch up to her, I plan to do something a lot more exciting than kiss the ground."

"It's about time."

* * *

Tracey waited until all the board members had filed into the conference room before making her entrance. Vincent Morelli dropped the gavel the moment he saw her sweep in, followed by office staff carrying printout materials that were placed in front of every member.

She'd dressed in an elegant black Italian designer suit, tailored yet incredibly chic and feminine. Black set off her tanned skin and red hair, which she'd had styled and tinted in New York to restore its original color. It was longer now and swished below her jawline.

Every male in the room sat up and took notice. Some of them gave her an unfriendly nod, others simply stared in shock that she'd dared to make an appearance in their all-male conclave.

For once in her life she felt totally confident. That was because she'd been tutored by Nikos, who was more brilliant, more successful than any of these obnoxious, arrogant financiers could ever hope to be.

"Mr. Chairman? I see no place for me at the table. Since I'm a member of this board, I suggest you do something about it immediately. And please provide me with a copy of today's agenda."

Vincent's face flamed with color before instructing the secretary to pull a chair over from the wall. It disturbed two of the men who had to rearrange their chairs to give her space.

She walked to the chair and sat down. An agenda was handed to her.

"Thank you."

Vincent was furious. She hadn't taken him up on his offer for dinner, and he hadn't been able to track her down. He finally got to his feet and cleared his throat. "Good morning gentlemen."

Tracey stood up. "There's a woman present."

His eyes shot sparks. "I was just going to say and Mrs. Von Axel."

"I've taken my maiden name back," she said in a clear voice. "Please address me as Ms. Conner. As a new member of this board, I wish to say a few words. If the secretary will please add my name to the list of today's agenda in the minutes."

"It's been duly noted," the secretary said before Vincent could object. Good. Not every member of the board was Morelli's puppet.

She sat down. The tension in the room was growing. She loved it. Welcomed it.

Vincent's hands spread like the pope's when he

was ready to bless his audience. "You have our attention, Ms. Conner. Go ahead and speak."

"You're out of order, Mr. Chairman. Please read the minutes, Mr. Secretary."

The chairman sent her another malevolent glance before the secretary began his task.

Thanks to Nikos she was able to digest the contents. Having studied the quarterly report, she'd already pinpointed the crux of the company's problem, which had started long before her grandfather had died.

The discussions at the last board meeting reflected its downward trend. She assumed solutions were going to be addressed at this one.

When he'd finished, he turned the meeting back over to Vincent, who looked around the room jerkily. "In view of Ms. Conner's unexpected presence here today, shall we cede the floor to her before getting down to business? All in favor?"

"I'm not!" She jumped to her feet. He was trying to railroad her the way her grandfather used to do, but he wasn't Paul Loretto. Because of Nikos, she no longer feared anyone. Staring Vincent down she said, "You're out of order again, Mr. Chairman."

She'd heard the term *apoplexy*. Vincent was doing a superb job of demonstrating it before his peers.

"According to the agenda, Mr. Rosenthal is first on the list." She nodded to the man across the table. "Go ahead."

He looked uncomfortable.

"Go on, Mr. Rosenthal," she prodded. "This isn't a police state. The chairman doesn't have the power to do anything. My grandfather appointed him, and this board let it happen. But this same board has the power to vote out a tyrant and put someone else in his place."

"How dare you!" Vincent's face had gone beet-red.

"Oh, I dare a lot more. Be careful what you say. I'd be more than happy to give them chapter and verse of a certain phone conversation with you seven weeks ago. But first I'd like to hear what idea Mr. Rosenthal has in mind to help the company, which has been failing for a long time."

She held her breath, waiting to see if anyone besides the secretary had a backbone. There was a hushed silence in the room before Mr. Rosenthal sat forward and began speaking.

The taste of victory was sweeter than she could have dreamed.

Oh Nikos. If only you were here to see what you've done…

One by one the men on the agenda made their comments. The secretary finally gave her the floor.

Tracey smiled. "Thank you, Mr. Secretary. I'd like it recorded in the minutes that the mansion I lived in all my life will be known from this day forward as the Emilio Loretto Center for Italians' in need. It will be kept up in its original state with all its art treasures intact. The deserving people who will live there will receive food, housing and financial aid toward higher education."

A collective gasp resounded in the room.

"Now for the rest of my business. As you're all aware, I own fifty-one percent of the company stock, which according to today's market figure stands at seven hundred million dollars. It's a little less than when Mother died seven weeks ago.

"Let it be noted in the minutes that I'm selling all my shares in order to finance the Loretto Center and two shelters. Thirty-six of them are earmarked to run the Mark and Diana Conner Foundation for abused women and children."

It did her heart good to see the way the men's faces froze at her use of the word *abused*. They all knew deep down what kind of a man her grandfather had been. He'd abused them!

"The proceeds from the sale of the other fifteen shares will be divided equally to run the center as well as support the Helios Foundation for abused animals."

Vincent remained uncharacteristically quiet.

"The way this board was set up, the current members have first option to buy my shares. Those of you with vision similar to mine have an opportunity to send this company in a new direction. For any transactions, please refer to my attorney Mr. Donald Jamison of Jamison, Mandrakey and Lowell in New York."

She wished she had a camera to preserve the astonished look on their faces. Nikos would love it.

"As my last order of business, let me announce that I'm resigning from this board as of today."

Another shock wave passed through the room.

"You won't be seeing me again. Therefore I ask your indulgence in considering the information before you. There isn't time for you to read it now. If you care about this company, you'll take the time when you can give it your full attention.

"Suffice it to say, the Loretto company founded by my ancesters could be better than it is. It should be better. Emilio didn't have the resources at his disposal we have in the twenty-first century.

"The vision of the company has been limited. It's true that mustard has been the flagship, but it can't do all the work as manifested by the drop in earnings.

"A wise man has taught me how to live the good life. The only way to repay him is to pass on some of his great knowledge to you. From him I've learned many things." She loved Nikos so much, it was a struggle to keep her voice steady. "This morning I want to talk about seeds."

Maybe she was wrong, but she felt the majority of the men were actually listening. Her confidence bloomed!

"Consider the flaxseed, for example. Research is proving that crushing it results in an ingredient that can be used to help the prostate and other organs fight cancer. In that one area alone, there's an untapped market.

"The material before you suggests several

possible markets I've investigated with potential revenue. Of course none of them could exist without the farmer who makes it all happen. Never forget that if Emilio hadn't stepped off a boat into the New World and helped grow tomato and mustard plants so he could stay alive, there'd be no Loretto's."

She took a satisfying breath. "That's all, gentlemen. Good luck in the future. I happen to believe in the next life. Nothing would give me greater pleasure than to meet Emilio one day and report that we'd been good stewards."

On that note, Tracey got up and walked out the door to the hall. She took the elevator to the ground floor and hurried from the building to the smoked-glass limo she had waiting with her luggage.

After she reached the Buffalo airport, she boarded a private charter for Geneva. A friend of Karl's had offered his chalet, where she planned to stay hidden from the paparazzi while she sorted out her future. One emptier than she could bear without Nikos. But she'd laid her last demon to rest and felt she could finally move on.

Once she was onboard the private jet and had

eaten lunch, she fell into a sound sleep. The buildup to the board meeting had exhausted her. She didn't waken until the steward told her to prepare for landing. An agent would be coming onboard to check her through customs.

After the plane touched down, she went into the bathroom to freshen up. When she emerged, she almost fainted to realize it was a Greek customs agent who'd entered the cabin asking to see her passport.

"Where am I?"

He smiled. "In Athens of course."

The suddenly pounding of her heart almost suffocated her. "But there's been a mistake— I'm supposed to be in Geneva!"

The agent shrugged and spread his hands before leaving.

Nikos?

This was *his* doing.

Naturally when the maids had gone to clean her hotel room, they'd told Maria she was gone, and one thing had led to another. Why would he go to all this trouble now?

Tracey couldn't face him again. She simply couldn't take the pain.

Frantic at this point, she turned to the steward. "Tell the captain to fly me to Geneva at once!"

"I'm sorry, Ms. Conner, but he has left the aircraft. There's a limo waiting for you at the bottom of the stairs. I took the liberty of putting your luggage inside. Whenever you're ready to deboard…"

Obviously Nikos wanted to know the outcome of the board meeting. She would have told him about it over the phone when she called him. But it appeared you didn't walk out on Nikos Lazaridis without a final goodbye face-to-face.

The walk into the conference room had been nothing compared to the short walk down the steps to the limo where she knew he was waiting. Her legs shook like jelly. The steward helped her in the back seat where she expected Nikos to be lounged there like a jungle cat.

But the limo was empty.

She sat back, presuming the driver was taking her to Nikos's condo. Instead she experienced déjà vu as it headed for the port of Piraeus, where her whole world had changed after bribing the waiter to bring Nikos to her.

Resigned to the inevitable, when the limo arrived

at the pier, she rode the waiting tender to a small white yacht anchored in the harbor. One of the crew helped her up the side steps to the deck.

"Welcome aboard, Tracey." A beaming Giorgios and Stella took turns hugging her.

"You're just in time for *your* wedding," his wife whispered before pinning a corsage to the shoulder of her suit jacket.

Giorgios reached for Tracey's hand and placed it on top of his arm. "Since your father isn't alive, may I have the honor of escorting you down the aisle? Nikos has grown impatient for this moment. Let's not keep him waiting any longer."

Beyond them she could see Nikos's family. Leon and Maria, Irena and Ari, the people she'd learned to love were here, assembled under a blue-and-white canopy. Standing in the front of them was a priest.

Next to him, dressed in formal dark wedding clothes, was the man who'd taken possession of her heart years ago. His eyes were smiling at her, beckoning her.

She knew instantly that he loved her the way she loved him. He knew everything, yet he still loved her.

This was a dream with no shadows. A wonderful, beautiful dream. Tracey found herself walking into it with her eyes wide open.

"Darling—" she sobbed for joy after a night of intense love making. The yacht had been at sea for hours. She barely felt the gentle motion as they lay entwined in the king-size bed below deck.

Nikos bent over her, kissing every inch of her face and hair. "Did I hurt you?" he cried in a voice full of concern. "I've wanted you for so long, I'm afraid I've worn you out."

She looked up at him in the semidarkness. "You know better than that." Her hands cupped his face. "I can't get enough of you because I love you too much. I'm afraid this kind of happiness is going to be snatched away from me."

He devoured her mouth once more. "After denying us joy all these years, the fates wouldn't be that cruel now. My gorgeous mermaid is finally beached in my private lagoon. I'm never letting you go."

Tracey brushed her lips against his. "You've called me that before."

He smiled, tracing the outline of her mouth

with his finger. "When I was outside the mansion, my eye caught sight of an enchanting young woman, beautifully formed, with a crown of long flowing red hair. You reminded me of a timid mermaid."

"I was hideous, darling."

"You're not a man, thank God, and you don't know what I saw. Every Greek boy grows up steeped in the myths of our heritage. We're warned to fight the pull of the Siren's call. If you sail too close, you're powerless to escape."

He kissed her again, longer and deeper. "When you smiled at me, you sent out a siren call I felt in every cell of my body. I couldn't believe a fifteen-year-old girl could make me weak with wanting. I wanted your heart.

"When I thought of you with Karl, it nearly destroyed me. I spent those seven years hating him and cursing you for making me love you so that I couldn't sustain a relationship with any other woman."

"Oh Nikos—" She slid her arms around his neck, crushing him to her. He rolled on his back, taking her with him. Now she could look down at him.

"I only have one heart, and I gave it to you that day. I think you know that by now."

His eyes turned molten, causing her to feel the full effect of his unslaked desire for her. That look made her breathless.

"The second I was free, I came to you, Nikos. Only you."

His strong legs trapped hers. "Don't ever stop coming to me, Tracey. Don't ever stop giving me your mouth and your body. I couldn't take it. There's this hunger in me to make every second count now."

"I know—those first two nights at the farm I felt reborn. It was then I realized what had been missing from my life without you. We've lost too many years. That's why I resigned from the board."

"Darling—" In the throes of intense emotion, he clasped her arms tighter.

"It's true. I had my day in court. It was glorious, and all because of you!" She crushed him in her arms, kissing him wildly. "I told them you taught me the meaning of the good life.

"You did, Nikos! With you I've felt reborn. The only thing I want out of life is to be a certain farmer's wife. Our children are going to have the greatest father on earth. We're all going to work together side by side and love each other. Comfort each other."

He stared hard at her. "You really mean it? You quit?"

"I did more than that. I announced I was giving all the money from my stock to two charities for the abused. One in my parents' names, and one called the Helios Foundation."

His eyes grew suspiciously bright.

"Then I told that bunch of sheep they would never see me again, and I walked out of there for good. Maybe some of them really aren't sheep. If enough of them can diminish Vincent's power, there might be hope for the company. Only time will tell.

"But the point is, as of this minute there'll be no more boardroom business for me. And something else. I no longer have a dime to my name."

He laughed that deep, rich male laugh she could feel to her very bones. She kissed his proud jaw.

"You're going to have to support me. But I'll help once my crop starts to make a profit. The first harvest is going to be my wedding present to you. Speaking of which, who is minding the crop while we're gone?"

"Leon said he'd keep an eye on it."

"But he hates farming."

"I know." He kissed her throat where a pulse throbbed. "Never underestimate the love of a great brother."

"Everything's really all right between the two of you?"

"Yes. Several weeks ago I had a serious talk with him. He admitted he was angry that I'd gone off by myself rather than stay in Kalambaka and work with him at the hotel.

"That's when I explained that I had a crush on Maria at the time, and hated seeing the two of them so happy together."

"You're kidding," Tracey cried.

"Leon thought I was kidding until I told him the real reason I never came home was because it wouldn't be home unless I brought you with me."

"Darling," she murmured against his lips, on fire with love for him.

"My explanation cleared away all the cobwebs. He actually broke down and cried. We're closer now than we've ever been in our lives.

"I told him Ari and I are alike in some ways. Maria was a beautiful woman, but she always loved Leon. Deep down I knew it, but my pride had a hard time handling it.

"When I saw Ari hanging around you, he reminded me too much of myself at that age. Leon accused me of being jealous of my own nephew. I'm afraid it's all true."

She smiled, kissing his nose. "Now everything's making sense."

"*Cherchez la femme*. All roads lead to a woman when you finally get down to the bottom of it. You've had me in your thrall from the beginning, Tracey."

On that note he pulled her to him and once again he was kissing her with a voracious appetite she hadn't even dreamed of.

The next time Tracey was awake, sunlight stole into the porthole. Her back lay against her husband's chest with his arms fastened around her. Even in sleep she felt his possessive hold and gloried in it.

Suddenly she felt him nibble her neck and earlobe.

"Oh good—I'm so glad you're awake!" She

turned over and threw herself at him, kissing him shamelessly.

He chuckled. "How long have you been this wide-eyed?"

"It has seemed like forever without you to play with," she teased.

His hands got enmeshed in her hair. "I think I know what's wrong."

"There's nothing wrong," she assured him.

"I do believe I've turned you into a farmer's wife. You're up with the sun. You couldn't be missing our farm, could you?"

"Well...now that you mention it..."

"You want me to tell the captain to turn the yacht around?"

"Oh no, darling—"

Laughter rolled out of him. "I miss the farm, too. And there's a little something missing you."

Tracey blinked. "What do you mean?"

"My wedding present to you. I'll phone Ari and ask him to bring it and a king-size bed to the house in the van so everything will be waiting for us when we get back tonight."

"I don't think I can wait that long to find out what it is."

"I'll give you a clue. It's black."

She let out a cry. "A puppy?"

His smile was so beautiful, it broke her heart. "A little male pug."

"Oh Nikos—I know what I'm going to name him—"

He grinned. "I do, too."

"That's because you're Helios and know everything."

His mouth covered hers in a deep, sensuous kiss. "You've got me believing it. Is there anything else you wanted?"

"No—" she said with her heart in her throat.

"What an easy woman to please." He gazed at her with adoring eyes. "I'm the luckiest of men. Come here to me," he whispered urgently.

"I don't think I can get any closer."

"Oh yes you can. Let me show you…"

MILLS & BOON PUBLISH EIGHT LARGE PRINT TITLES A MONTH. THESE ARE THE EIGHT TITLES FOR NOVEMBER 2007.

BOUGHT: THE GREEK'S BRIDE
Lucy Monroe

THE SPANIARD'S BLACKMAILED BRIDE
Trish Morey

CLAIMING HIS PREGNANT WIFE
Kim Lawrence

CONTRACTED: A WIFE FOR THE BEDROOM
Carol Marinelli

THE FORBIDDEN BROTHER
Barbara McMahon

THE LAZARIDIS MARRIAGE
Rebecca Winters

BRIDE OF THE EMERALD ISLE
Trish Wylie

HER OUTBACK KNIGHT
Melissa James

MILLS & BOON®
Pure reading pleasure

1007 Rom LP

MILLS & BOON PUBLISH EIGHT LARGE PRINT TITLES A MONTH. THESE ARE THE EIGHT TITLES FOR DECEMBER 2007.

TAKEN: THE SPANIARD'S VIRGIN
Lucy Monroe

THE PETRAKOS BRIDE
Lynne Graham

THE BRAZILIAN BOSS'S INNOCENT MISTRESS
Sarah Morgan

FOR THE SHEIKH'S PLEASURE
Annie West

THE ITALIAN'S WIFE BY SUNSET
Lucy Gordon

REUNITED: MARRIAGE IN A MILLION
Liz Fielding

HIS MIRACLE BRIDE
Marion Lennox

BREAK UP TO MAKE UP
Fiona Harper

MILLS & BOON
Pure reading pleasure